The People Next Door

Also by Caroline Crane

Summer Girl
The Girls Are Missing
Coast of Fear
Wife Found Slain
The Foretelling
The Third Passenger
Woman Vanishes
Trick or Treat
Something Evil
Someone at the Door
Circus Day
The Man in the Shadows

THE PEOPLE NEXT DOOR

A Novel of Suspense

CAROLINE CRANE

DODD, MEAD & COMPANY
New York

Copyright ©1988 by Caroline Crane

All rights reserved.
No part of this book may be reproduced in any form
without permission in writing from the publisher.
Published by Dodd, Mead & Company, Inc.
71 Fifth Avenue, New York, New York 10003.
Manufactured in the United States of America.

The People Next Door

CHAPTER 1

Debra Gillis opened the car window and let the June breeze blow over her face. The air conditioner was on, but its benefits did not reach the back seat where she rode drowsing beside her young son.

Gigi, her fifteen-year-old stepdaughter, sat in front with Kurt and watched for glimpses of the ocean as they drove down the Garden State Parkway to their new home. Kurt had warned her that there would be no glimpses. The parkway was too far inland.

Gigi turned around and fixed Debra with a glare.

"I hope you people realize," she told them all, "the only reason I decided to spend the summer with you is you're going to be at the beach. Otherwise I'd have stayed with my mom."

"We're aware of that," said Kurt.

"Of course," agreed Debra. She knew very well that Gigi wasted no love on her. It had not been necessary to drive the point home.

Gigi added, "I don't mean to hurt your feelings or anything, but you know." It was a plea for understanding, addressed to her father.

He nodded. He was probably the only one who didn't know. For he was charmed by Gigi, and refused to see the problems she created.

No, thought Debra sorrowfully but fairly, it wasn't only Gigi. The real trouble was that they were too close in age. Debra was only eleven years older, hardly enough for any real authority.

"Dad, remember, you promised me surf," Gigi said. "Real waves. You'd better be right."

"What makes you think I'm not?" he asked.

"I looked at the map and there's this sort of sandbar that goes all the way down the shore. There's places out on that, but Luna Beach isn't one of them."

"If you looked at the map," Kurt replied, "you should have noticed that the sandbar, or whatever you call it, doesn't go all the way north. Luna Beach is above it."

"But then you run into Sandy Hook and Staten Island and things."

"Trust me. I've been there."

"To see the college?" she asked.

"And rent the house."

"Do you guarantee there are waves? I don't want to swim in any piddling old bay."

"When I was there in March," he assured her, "the waves were phenomenal. That was March. If they haven't settled down, I don't think any of us will do much swimming."

"I will," Gigi muttered, and lapsed into silence. Debra wondered how they would endure the summer.

But even three months with a difficult teenager was a small price to pay for getting away from Long Island. From that pushy redhead, Stacie Whatever-her-name-was, who had Kurt wrapped around her finger.

Debra had never told him that she knew about the girl. A graduate student. Some sort of assistant in his department. It was better to pretend ignorance, she thought. Otherwise things might get out of hand. She had heard of women who found themselves divorced when all they had really wanted was their righteous indignation.

Gigi rested her arm across the back of the seat. "Are you going to be teaching all day?" she asked her father. "Every day?"

Her voice was plaintive. She did not want to be stuck at home with Debra.

"Pretty much," he said. "It's my job, kiddo. It pays for the groceries and the house near the beach."

"How near?" Gigi asked.

"I told you, didn't I? Two blocks and a park."

"A big park?"

"Just a sliver."

Debra tuned out their voices and watched the parkway go by, while beside her little Drew nodded and dozed in his safety seat. She had never questioned that she would sit in back with him, giving up the place beside Kurt to his daughter. She did not think of Drew and Gigi as "the children." Instead she thought of Drew and herself as "us."

Gigi chattered on. "Dad, can I go to the college with you sometimes?"

"Maybe," he said. "But what's the hurry? You'll be in college yourself soon enough."

"You've got to be kidding. Two years is ages. Can I listen in on your lectures?"

"I guess so, if they allow it. And if Chaucer turns you on." He looked over his shoulder. "How's the kid doing back there?"

"Sleeping," said Debra.

"Thank God."

She winced. She did her best with Drew, trying to curb his all-too-frequent tantrums. Kurt said she spoiled him. She tried to remind him that Drew was in the "terrible twos." Kurt could not remember what Gigi had been like at two.

"Looks as if we're getting there." Kurt had seen an exit sign.

Gigi asked, "How did you ever find a house to rent?"

"Through an agent."

"Yes, but I mean what sort of people have houses to rent? I should think they'd either live in it or sell it."

"People have their reasons," he said. "It's a family that owns a corner lot with two houses. Quite a good-sized lot. They used to live in the big house and rent out the smaller one. Now they've decided to switch."

"How come?"

He was busy changing lanes and did not answer. Debra said, "Maybe their children grew up."

Gigi kept her eyes fixed on her father as though Debra did not exist.

"I don't think it was quite that," said Kurt. "I had the impression that something happened to their child. I'm not quite sure. It was just an allusion he made."

"What did he say?" Gigi asked.

"I really don't remember. It was a passing remark. But I got the feeling it was a pretty final happening."

Debra closed the window to hear him better. "Not their only child, I hope."

Gigi glowered at her. "What difference does it make?"

"Seems to me it might have been," Kurt replied. "I really didn't ask, you know. I was there to rent a house, not poke my nose into family business."

4

"Well, I just thought—" Debra began.

How could she explain? She only wanted to know because she cared. It must be terrible to lose a child.

Kurt turned onto an exit ramp and paid another toll. "Gigi, get out the map and tell me where I'm going. It's all marked."

Gigi acquired instant expertise in the art of map-reading and guided her father, with only a few errors, to the borough of Luna Beach.

He stopped at a downtown office to pick up the housekey, then made his way to Barton Avenue and drove slowly along it while Gigi read out the street names. At Angel Road he pulled into a driveway. They were home.

It neither looked nor felt like home. It was an old house, large and white with a mansard roof. It had a bay window in the living room and a front porch well shaded by a large-leafed vine.

"It's right on the street," Debra said in dismay. Worse than that, it was an intersection, just when Drew was at the age of great mobility and little sense.

"There's a setback," Kurt pointed out. "And they're fairly quiet streets. That vine should help to muffle the traffic noises."

"Kurt, I'm talking about your son."

"You'll have to watch him, that's all." Kurt and Gigi got out of the car. Debra opened the door, but did not want to leave Drew, who still slept.

Despite its being a populated area, the place had an attractive ruralness about it. Perhaps it was the gracious old house, or the rose-covered rail fence that surrounded the lot.

There were flowers everywhere. Beds of low blooms bordered the driveway and the concrete walk. Hydrangea bushes grew in front of the porch. She was glad the gardens were already established but supposed she would have to keep them free of weeds.

Gigi cried, "There's the park, and I can see the ocean! I can really see it, right from here! Oh, Dad, this is cool. I love it!" She hugged her father and he patted her back.

They were so alike, Debra thought. Both blond, with clean-cut features. While Kurt's were preppily handsome, Gigi's were dainty and pretty, and her cheeks dimpled when she smiled.

Drew took after his mother, with brown eyes and a shock of thick, dark hair. His was a shade lighter than hers, and silky soft. Gently she brushed her cheek across it, then lifted him from his seat. He woke with an irritable wail and a frenzy of kicking.

"Hush, Drewie," she crooned. "We're at our new house now. Don't you want to see the new house?" She tried to set him down, but he clung stickily to her neck.

Kurt had unlocked the house and gone inside with Gigi. Debra carried Drew around to see the back. She found a grassy yard shaded by a giant oak tree. Next to the driveway, an unused vegetable patch had been allowed to go to weed.

The driveway continued on past a weathered picket fence. Beyond it, partly hidden behind heavy shrubbery, was the other, smaller house.

There was something almost tropically garish about it. Salmon pink walls and a dark green roof rose above a riot of foliage and flowers. The only sign of human habitation was an umbrella clothesline near the fence. Sheets, pillowcases, and men's underwear rippled in the warm sea breeze.

Drew squirmed in her arms. "Get down."

She set him onto the grass. "This is where you're going to play, Drewie. It's your very own yard. Maybe we can get you a sandbox. Wouldn't that be fun?"

She would have liked a swing set, too, but there were limits, when they did not have plans for staying more than a year. They had not given up their apartment on Long Island, but only sublet it, on the chance that they might return. It would depend upon how Kurt liked Luna College. And, although he had never said so, on how the college liked him.

She hoped they would stay. It was a better place for Drew than an apartment.

A door slammed and Kurt called, "Hey, where are you? Don't you want to see the house?"

"I was showing Drew the yard," she said. "But I wish it were fenced."

"Come and help me unload the car. I want to get it out of the way before the movers come. We'll have to remember to keep the driveway clear so the Mauls can get in and out."

"Is that their name?" Debra asked. "Like what grizzly bears do?"

"It's a perfectly respectable name." He took their suitcases from the car and ushered her in through the back door. "Voilà the kitchen."

It was spacious, much larger than the one in their old apartment. Its windows looked out on the backyard and the other house.

He pointed to a closed door. "That's the way to the basement." And an open one. "That's supposed to be the maid's suite, I assume. Bedroom and bath."

Gigi emerged from the maid's suite. "I'm having this room. Dad said it's okay."

It sounded like a challenge, but Debra felt relieved that Gigi would not be upstairs with them.

They went on into the dining room. From there, French doors opened into the living room, where there was a large fireplace.

A faint smell of cold ashes permeated the room. There were long, lace-curtained windows, but the porch outside kept it pleasantly shaded. She wondered how their modern furniture would look in such a place.

"After the summer," Kurt confided, "that downstairs room of Gigi's is going to be my study."

"What about before that?"

"I'll use one of the upstairs rooms."

"How many are there?"

"Four upstairs and one down. And three bathrooms. We could open a bed and breakfast."

"I'm not surprised the people wanted to move out," she said. "It wouldn't make sense if you didn't have kids. But I wonder why they didn't sell the whole property. They probably could have gotten a fortune."

She babbled, trying to suppress her uneasiness. There was something about the house that bothered her. It might have been the size, or possibly the strangeness. Yet always before she had enjoyed new places and experiences.

She took Drew's hand and they followed Kurt up the stairs.

The second floor was divided by a hallway with two rooms on either side. The master bedroom was at the front of the house and had its own bath. The room next to it was smaller than the other two. All had white ruffled curtains in the windows.

Debra studied each room, trying to decide which would be best for Drew. She wanted him near her. Close enough so she could hear him if he called out or tried to wander.

"Which room do you want, Drewie?" she asked.

He buried his face against her leg. "Don't like it."

"What don't you like?"

"Don't like it *here*."

"You'll get used to it. It's just different, that's all."

She tried to reassure him, but her own negative feelings had not left her.

Maybe it was simply Kurt's story that disturbed her, about the Mauls' child, to whom something terrible had happened. Or maybe it was the unfamiliar, alien smell of the place.

Downstairs it had been the fireplace. Here it was not quite a smell, but more of an aura, as though the house had been closed for a long time. Perhaps it was simply the accumulation of someone else's life. She went from room to room, opening the windows and letting in fresh air.

The rooms at the front faced east, where they would get the morning sun. That would wake Drew up too early. She chose one of the others, directly across the hall from where she and Kurt would be.

"How do you like this room?" she asked. "It's bigger than the one you had back home. Pretty soon your bed will be here, and your toy box, and we'll fix you up a nice place to play. I'll put a rug on the floor so you won't get splinters."

"Don't like it," Drew said again.

"But, honey, this is home now." She sat down on the windowsill and gathered him into her arms.

The sill was low and the window gaped wide, leading straight down to the yard below. They would need some kind of lock or stop on the sash. Better yet, a guardrail.

Kurt bellowed from downstairs, "Hey, Debra! What did you do, fall asleep up there?"

Still carrying Drew, she went down to the kitchen. Kurt had brought in the cooler with their perishable food.

"Better get this stuff in the refrigerator," he said. "Gigi and I are going to pick up some cold beer for the movers."

"Could you get some milk for Drew?" she asked. "And,

Kurt, if you see a hardware store, we're going to need windowguards upstairs."

"What for? Do you think burglars will be climbing up the drainpipe?"

"I'm not talking about burglars. I mean Drew. There's nothing to keep him from falling out."

"I grew up in a place like this and it didn't have windowguards," Kurt said with some annoyance. "Did you have windowguards when you were a kid?"

"I don't think so. But part of the time we lived in a ranch house."

"It's just not necessary. If you're in an apartment on the eighteenth floor, yes. But here—"

Gigi tittered. Debra looked from one to the other. They thought she was being ridiculous, the way she hovered over Drew.

"All right, forget it," she said. "I just hope nothing happens."

Gigi murmured, "I never fell out a window. And we didn't have guards."

"I'm glad," said Debra. "But boys are more adventurous. You know that."

"I never did, either," Kurt put in.

She hated it when they ganged up on her. "Go get your beer," she told them, and opened the cooler. "And don't forget to buy milk."

After they left, she inspected the kitchen to see if anything needed cleaning. The cupboards were immaculate, the shelves freshly papered. The refrigerator had been scoured. There was nothing for her to do but put away the food and air the cooler.

Drew came toward her, humming as he ran his plastic truck along the edge of the countertop. She caught him and hugged him.

"I love you so much," she whispered.

He wriggled away from her and went back to his toy. The days of dependent babyhood were already gone. He was his own person now. It was a bittersweet realization.

The sound of the doorbell made her jump. Probably the movers, she thought.

A middle-aged woman in a flowered dress stood on the step outside. She was ash blond and slender, maybe a little too thin. She wore white button earrings and a choker of white plastic beads.

"I'm Enid Maul," the woman said. "You must be Mrs. Gillis?"

"Yes, I am." Debra stood back to admit her. "You're our landlady, right?"

The woman smiled faintly. "You could call it that. I just wanted to be sure everything's all right."

"It seems to be. It's all so nice and clean. I was just putting our stuff in the refrigerator."

"If you need anything, or have any questions, give me a call. Here's my number." She handed Debra a piece of paper with a telephone number on it. "Is your husband here?"

"No, he went to get some beer for the movers."

The woman's eyes moved almost unwillingly to Drew. Her lips tightened and she quickly looked away.

"Well, if you need anything . . ." She started down the steps.

"Thank you," Debra called after her. "It was nice to meet you."

Mrs. Maul got into her car and drove on out to the street.

It had been an odd encounter, Debra thought. So brief. Maybe she had to get somewhere in a hurry.

But the way she had looked at Drew . . . It was downright hostile. How could any woman look at a baby that way?

And what had happened to her own child? Was it the ocean? The traffic?

There were so many things. Life was so fragile.

Debra shuddered as something dark seemed to pass over her. She snatched up Drew and, unmindful of his protests, held him tightly.

CHAPTER 2

"I didn't want to come here," Enid Maul told the doctor. "It was my sister's idea, but I don't think there's anything you can do."

Nervously she toyed with the handle of her shiny white pocketbook, squeezing it into a loop around her finger. Lois was wrong. She should not have made the appointment. It was going to cost a lot of money and not do any good.

"Why don't we talk about it?" the doctor suggested. "Often it helps just to talk things over."

"That's why my sister sent me. She got tired of hearing me talk about it, and my husband won't listen, and everybody says it's my fault."

"Who's your sister?" he asked.

"Her name's Lois Claridge. She met you at a party a couple of months ago. Short blond hair, roundish face. Well, anyway."

The doctor listened soberly, as though she were saying something important. He was no older than forty, she thought. Lean, reptilian, self-satisfied.

13

She really wished she hadn't come. There was something disgraceful in having to see a psychiatrist. It meant you couldn't handle it yourself. Lois had said, "You'd go to a doctor if you broke your leg, wouldn't you? Nobody'd expect you to handle that yourself."

"How come," she asked, stalling for time, "your name is Longwort without an h? What happened to the h?"

"I don't know," he said. "Is there supposed to be an h?"

"Isn't it usually Longworth?"

"Possibly. That might be a little prettier, mightn't it?" He smiled.

It was all the same to him if they never got to the point. He would still collect his fee. It made her angry.

She fingered the choker around her neck. Those people had a child. A little child. And that made her angry, too.

"My new tenants have a child," she said.

He nodded. His silence forced her to continue talking.

"I stopped by there on my way over. I thought I could handle it, but now I'm not sure. I don't know what I'm going to do if I can't handle it. They have a year's lease."

"A lot of people have children," he said. "Children are all over the place. Is there any particular reason why you think you can't handle it?"

"Of course there's a reason!"

Lois had said she discussed it with him, but how could he be expected to remember?

"Last February—" She pressed her knuckles to her mouth. "My son . . . He took a gun and shot himself. My only child."

"I see."

"And I don't even know where he got the gun." Her voice broke. She drew a long, shuddering breath.

The doctor let her cry for a moment, then asked, "Do you want to tell me about it?"

She wiped away her tears. "There's nothing to tell. It happened. And nobody can change that."

"Nobody can change the past," he agreed, "but we can try to change things for you. You're entitled to the best life possible, even under the circumstances."

She stared at him with watery eyes. "How? That's just crazy. Unless you give me amnesia. Can you do that?"

"Not quite, Enid, but we can—"

"I'd rather be called Mrs. Maul. I don't like it when doctors use first names. It's patronizing. Besides, I think I'm older than you."

"I'm thirty-nine," he said. "Of course, you can have it the way you like, but most of my patients call me Charlie. It breaks down the barriers."

"That's another thing I don't like is being considered a patient. I'm not sick. And I'd rather be called Mrs. Maul." She was suddenly, violently put off by the fact that he was three years younger. How could Lois have done such a thing? Of course, Lois was younger, too, the same age as he, so she probably hadn't thought about it. Besides, Lois looked up to doctors.

"Anyway," she said, "there's nothing you can do. I just want somebody to tell me why. I don't understand. Why couldn't he talk to me?"

"Did he leave a note?" asked the doctor. "Did he say anything beforehand? Talk about death, for instance?"

She shook her head. "It was so sudden. I thought he was doing all right. In college. His first year. He lived at home, but he had a car."

She forgot what she was saying. Forgot everything except that silent house, with Billy's car parked outside, and the terrible feeling that something was wrong.

"I don't understand it." Her eyes kept flooding and she

hiccupped softly. The doctor held out a box of yellow Kleenex. She took one.

"Did it happen at home?" he asked.

"In the basement. It's a finished basement. A family room." She sobbed again.

"How did you find out?"

"I *saw* him. I came home . . . I work in my husband's office part time. He has a real estate and insurance business. I got home and Billy's car was there. I thought he'd be in the house, but everything was quiet. He was always playing his records."

She sniffled, and dabbed at her eyes. "I couldn't help thinking something was wrong. It was just a feeling I had. I'm his mother."

The doctor nodded.

"Then I saw the basement door was open, and it was cold."

She watched the scene unfold like a movie. It was a picture she had seen many times.

"The basement has its own heater," she explained. "When people are down there they turn it on, but we don't leave it on. It's too expensive. And Frank always told him to keep the door shut so it wouldn't drain heat from the rest of the house."

"Frank is—?"

"My husband. Anyway, there was the door open and only cold air coming up. I went down to see. I just felt something was wrong."

The doctor gave her a moment, then asked, "It couldn't have been an accident?"

"How?" Enid demanded. "He wasn't cleaning the gun, or anything. They could tell that. I don't know where he got it. I never saw it before, but I don't go around snooping. It wasn't registered. They checked. One of those Saturday night specials. I can't see Billy having a gun like that."

She could not see Billy using it, either, on himself or anyone else. Possibly only for target practice. But not in the basement.

"How was he doing in school?" asked the doctor.

"Okay, I guess."

"What about his social life? Any girlfriends?"

"Some. I mean, he dated, but there was nothing really serious."

"Did he talk to you about things like that? Or about school?"

"He used to, but not when he got older."

"Did he talk to his father?"

"Billy was always closer to me. Frank didn't get so involved. And he criticized him a lot. He criticizes me, too, and now he blames me—"

A flicker of interest lit the doctor's face. "So your son was close to you?"

"Closer to me than Frank, but he had his own friends. The police asked everybody. Billy never talked about suicide."

"Did he talk about death? Were there any disappointments? A broken romance? Did he have any problem with drugs or alcohol that you know of?"

"No, Doctor, there was no *reason*."

The doctor crossed his legs and settled back in his overstuffed chair. He was tall and thin and reminded her of a camel, with an aloof, superior expression. Even his hair was tawny and wiry like a camel's, but the green eyes, sleepily watchful, came straight from a snake.

"Did you notice any change in your son's behavior?" he asked. "His habits?"

"I guess so, about five years ago," Enid replied. "I thought it was the usual teenage stuff. He got fresh, he got messy, he stayed out later than we said. He scarcely talked to his father, but Frank's not always easy to talk to."

"How do you and your husband get along? Is it a pretty good marriage?"

"Not really. We're not . . . friends. With some couples, the husband and wife are best friends. I can't tell Frank anything. And sometimes he cheats on me. I know it, but he thinks I don't."

"Was it always like that?"

"Not in the beginning. Unless I was living in a dream world. But we didn't fight. At least not in front of Billy. We were always careful about that."

"That's not why I asked," he said. "You mentioned the closeness you had with your son. I've found that a person in a poor marital situation, where there's not much emotional intimacy between the spouses, will sometimes look for that closeness with the children, often one child in particular. It answers an emotional need and also a narcissistic one. The person may in some ways try to bind the child to him. Or her."

"I never did that!" she cried. "I wanted him to grow up normal, and have girlfriends, and get married . . . I *never* did anything like that."

"Mrs. Maul, please. I didn't mean it in a sexual way. People like that need to see themselves reflected in someone's eyes as attractive and desirable."

"That *is* sexual."

"Not necessarily."

"Anyway, it's not true," she wept. "It was because of Frank. Billy's sensitive and couldn't take his hounding. Frank's a difficult person. But he can be awfully attractive."

"What sort of things did he criticize about Billy?"

"Everything. Frank thinks people should do things his way. He wanted Billy to play football and get in with the social crowd. He made fun of him when he didn't. And when Billy started driving, Frank would yell at him even before he made a mistake. And the parking tickets . . ."

"Parking tickets?"

"You know how crowded this town gets, especially in summer. It's hard to find a place. Frank has a parking lot behind his office, but he wouldn't let Billy use it because he might crowd out a customer. So Billy'd park by a fire hydrant, or in front of a driveway, or he'd let his meter expire. After the first time, I didn't tell Frank. I paid the fines myself."

"Why didn't Billy pay them?"

"He was in school. He didn't have that kind of money."

"What kind of money are we talking about?" The doctor hooked one leg over the arm of his chair. "Haven't you ever wondered why he racked up so many fines, especially if you paid them?"

"He was careless, that's all."

"Nobody's just careless, Mrs. Maul. He was trying to tell you something. If he knew you were paying the fines, and he kept on running them up, that was hostility. Didn't you realize you were being punished?"

"For . . . what?"

"For not letting him go."

"I did let him go! I never—"

"Physically, maybe, but emotionally you kept him bound."

"You're saying it's my fault he shot himself! Isn't that what you're saying?" She groped for the Kleenex box. He pushed it toward her.

"You're just like . . . all of them," she wept. "Frank, my sister, the neighbors . . . There isn't a person on Angel Road who cares that my heart is broken. They're all too busy telling me what I did wrong." She blotted her eyes and blew her nose with a mass of sodden yellow tissues.

"Did you say Angel Road?" he asked.

"Angel and Barton. It's where I live."

"You've had quite a lot going on over there, haven't you?"

She looked up, glad to change the subject. "Do you mean the break-ins? They're all over. Anywhere there's summer houses. I think it's drugs."

"Break-ins, yes," he said. "But wasn't there some tragedy on the beach? Something to do with a small child?"

"Well, it's right near the water. And some mothers don't know how to watch their children."

"As I recall, it was last January. Not very likely a child would be in the water at that time of year, is it?" His snake eyes held a glint of triumph.

"You never know about kids," she said vaguely.

"And it seems to me," he went on, "that it wasn't exactly a drowning. I believe the child's neck was broken. They never did find out what happened, did they?"

"Not as far as I know," said Enid. "What's your point?"

"I'm sorry, I was digressing." He looked at his watch. "It seems our time is almost up."

She wondered if he was disappointed. He believed they were just getting into something.

"Well," she said, "I don't think we accomplished very much, except that I feel worse than when I came in."

He smiled. "I'm sorry to hear that. What's the matter, can't you take constructive criticism?"

She stared at him in amazement. "How can it be constructive when it's too *late*? You can't give me back those years. None of you can, so why do you keep piling it on?"

"Why is it so important to you?" he asked. "What do you care what other people think?"

She sniffled and dried her eyes, but more tears came. "It's

bad enough knowing what a failure I am, without everybody rubbing it in."

"Do you think you're a failure, Mrs. Maul?"

"I must be, if my own son wanted to kill himself." She seized another handful of tissues. "It's my punishment. I was so proud when he was born."

"Most parents are proud."

"Mine always wanted a boy. But they had two girls and I got the boy. I had something my mother wanted that she couldn't get. And my sister, too. She has two girls."

"You seem to feel a lot of rivalry there," he observed.

"I already know that. My mother was very insecure and so am I, but anyway . . ."

"Then this rage you have is probably a displacement of your anger at your mother."

"Not quite," said Enid. "Some of it's where it belongs. But I do displace a lot. I already know that."

"On to mother figures," he said with a grin. Meaning himself, no doubt, and Lois. Even Frank.

"On to mothers," she said. "And their children, especially little children. Everything I had has been taken away from me. Even my happy memories. It's all discredited. It's worthless, because I made such a mess of it."

"Then you're really angry at yourself."

"Maybe, but I'm jealous of them. Of mothers who are just starting out. They haven't lost their chance and maybe they never will, and they're so damn smug. It makes me bitter. I can't even stand the sight of those kids. And that's not normal, is it?"

"We can talk about it," said the doctor.

"Sure. I'll call you."

She never would. He probably knew it. And he would think

it was because she couldn't face the truth about herself.

She went out to her car, which was dotted with bird droppings. She had parked under a tree. Absently she rubbed at them with the damp tissues still in her hand, and wondered how anybody could really know the truth.

CHAPTER 3

Kurt was busy with the movers, showing them where to put the furniture. Debra kept Drew in the backyard, out of the way.

The yard was shady and comfortable. Whatever unpleasant aura was in the house did not seem to reach her there. Even Drew was content.

Gigi, in one of her good moods, came and flopped down on the grass beside them.

"Guess what. I went over to look at the beach and I met some gorgeous guys. One of them lives right here on the next block. He used to know the Maul boy."

"I suppose people would," said Debra. "It's not a big city."

"Aren't you even interested? I found out what happened."

"All right, tell me." Debra bent over to tighten Drew's shoelace. Childishly, she refused to give in to Gigi's excitement.

"He shot himself," Gigi said. "Right here in our house, in the basement. Almost blew his head off. No wonder they didn't want to stay."

"When was that?" Debra could not imagine such a thing. She had pictured a young child. Like Drew.

"Last winter. February. And you know what? This whole place must be jinxed. A little before that, they found a kid dead on the beach. Three years old. It was a boy who lived on Angel Road. Billy Maul used to baby-sit him. Todd knew him, too. Todd's the cute guy I met."

"What a terrible thing." Debra wondered if that could have been the cause of Billy Maul's suicide. Teenagers were known to be extravagant in their reactions. Sometimes fatally so.

"How old was he?" she asked. "I mean the Maul boy?"

"I don't know. About Todd's age, I guess. Eighteen or nineteen. They said the story about that kid was in all the papers back then. He disappeared right out of his bed at night." Gigi rested her chin on her knees and watched Drew sailing his toy boats in the grass.

Debra looked up at the house. It had given her a bad feeling. Now she knew. Billy's suicide might have had a more sinister reason than grief . . .

"Why don't you let him use real water?" Gigi asked. "You wouldn't have to worry about it spilling out here."

Debra pulled herself together. "I would, if I could find a container. Everything's still packed.'

"I want water!" Drew banged his boat on the ground.

"This is pretend water," Debra told him. "The grass is your water."

"I want *water*." He began to kick.

Gigi laughed. "I didn't think he'd understand." She jumped up and held out her hand. "Want to take a walk with me, Drewie? Let's go see the real water. Is that okay?"

"I guess so," Debra said reluctantly. "But keep him out of it, will you? And please don't let go of him, whatever you do."

Gigi tossed her a scowl and set off down the driveway, with Drew's hand clutched dutifully in hers. Debra watched, her heart torn at the sight of his eager, toddling walk. She realized that part of her trouble was jealousy. She wanted him all to herself. Wanted his total allegiance.

She went around to the front of the house where the moving van was still parked. Two men unloaded it while two others tramped in and out of the house carrying cartons and small objects. The larger pieces were already in place.

She was about to go inside when a car turned in at the driveway.

It was not Enid Maul's, but a blue station wagon. The driver, a woman with short blond hair, surveyed the van blocking her way, then backed out and parked at the curb. She returned on foot, accompanied by two young girls.

Debra apologized for the inconvenience. "I'm really sorry about all this. They should be finished in a little while."

"No problem," said the woman. "You must be Enid's new tenants. I'm her sister, Lois Claridge. Do you happen to know if she's home?"

"I don't think so," Debra replied. "I saw her go out a while ago and she hasn't come back."

"Oh, she must be at that place," Lois said vaguely.

One of the girls groaned. "Do we have to go there?"

"No, we'll wait." Their mother seemed content to stay with Debra. "You can go on over to the house, but you can't get in. Aunt Enid always locks up."

The girls skipped away. They were both preadolescent with long, thin legs. One had the beginnings of a bust.

"I don't know if anyone told you," Lois said, "but there have been a few burglaries around here. It's mostly the summer houses when they're empty, but I thought you'd want to know not to leave things open. You're . . . Enid mentioned your name, but I—"

"I'm sorry. Debra Gillis. You just missed my little boy. And my stepdaughter. They went for a walk. My husband's inside."

"How old is your stepdaughter?"

"She's fifteen."

"Oh." Lois seemed disappointed. "My kids would be a little young. Vicky's twelve and Robin's ten." She stared thoughtfully after the girls. "They're just getting to the age . . ."

Debra wondered what she was supposed to say. That she had noticed?

But Lois went on. "Some of them start even younger. Even the grade schools have a drug problem now, especially with crack. And it's bad in this town, where there are so many young people. You know, because of the beach. They all come here for that. It's a scene. If you have a fifteen-year-old daughter, you might want to keep an eye on her."

"Fortunately," said Debra, "she's only here for the summer, but thanks for warning me. I don't know what I can do, though. I can't keep her under lock and key."

"Just watch for the signs," Lois advised. "And watch who her friends are. That usually tells a lot."

They went around to the backyard. Debra regretted that there was nothing to sit on.

"We lived in an apartment before, so we don't have outdoor furniture," she explained.

They both sat on the grass.

"Where did you live?" asked Lois.

"Long Island. My husband taught college there. He's on a leave of absence. We might go back when this year is over."

"What does he teach?"

"Early English literature. Chaucer and things. He's working on a book, but I doubt if he'll ever finish it."

Debra looked over at the Mauls' house. She could not forget what Gigi had told her, or her own speculations.

"I met your sister," she ventured, "a while ago. She stopped by on her way out."

"Oh. Yes. Well, you probably won't see much of her. She keeps to herself a lot."

Debra took a plunge. "I heard about the terrible thing that happened . . ."

"Yes, it was awful. Poor Enid. She hasn't been the same."

"Who would be? Was that . . . Were there any other children?"

"No, but I don't know if that would matter. Each child is special, don't you think? Is that your husband?"

Kurt had opened the kitchen window. "Hi, how are you?" he said to Lois. Debra introduced them.

Kurt smiled charmingly. "Sorry to bother you, but we need some traveler's checks. The movers are almost finished."

"I'll be right there." Debra scrambled to her feet. "I'm the one who got the checks, so I have to sign them. It's been very nice meeting you."

"I'll see you again." Lois stood up and brushed off her slacks. "Take care."

Debra paid the movers and then took a tour of the house. It looked raw and unsettled, with cartons stacked against the walls. She had her work cut out for her, but it was worth it to give Drew a yard to play in, and to get away from Kurt's redhead on Long Island.

Drew's room was a disaster. Kurt had placed the bed under a window. She wondered how he could have been so stupid, especially after denying that they needed windowguards. Pulling and tugging, she rearranged every piece of furniture. When she went back downstairs, the van had left and Kurt was drinking a beer.

"Where are the kids?" he asked.

"They went for a walk. I hope Gigi doesn't let him go in the water. She just finished telling me about a child who drowned there."

"When, today?"

"No, last winter sometime. You know Gigi. She went out for a walk and she'll start a conversation with anybody. I think you should tell her, Kurt."

"Tell her what?"

"Not to be so trusting. Do you want to go and see if we can find them?"

"Why not?" He tossed away his beer can.

"We'd better lock up," she said. "Lois told me there are a lot of burglaries."

"Can't get away from it, can we?" He checked to be sure he had the key.

They crossed Barton Avenue and walked toward the foot of Angel Road, which ended at the park. Even from a distance, she could see waves. Real waves, as Gigi had wanted, but deadly for a small child.

"Why so quiet?" asked Kurt. "Oh, well, you're usually pretty quiet."

As though it were a fault.

"I was thinking about the child who drowned," she said. "He wasn't much older than Drew."

"Why do you want to dwell on a thing like that? Why not think about all the children who don't drown?"

He was right. She really should do that. "It just scares me sometimes. So many things can happen."

"A little caution's okay," he told her, "but let's not get neurotic about it."

"I am neurotic about it. I can't help it. And after what Gigi told me . . . Did you know the Maul boy committed suicide? Right in our basement. He shot himself."

"Suicide, huh? You girls have been busy since we got here, digging up the dirt."

"Yes, well, you can thank Gigi. But we probably would have found out sooner or later."

They walked through the small strip of park to a flight of steps that led down into the sand. The beach seemed crowded, although it was still only June. There were flocks of teenagers. Gigi would have a wonderful time. There were mothers and children, vacationers, retirees. Very few were actually swimming. The water was probably still bone-chilling.

"How are you going to find them?" asked Kurt.

Gigi had been wearing white shorts and a hot pink T-shirt. Squinting in the sunlight, Debra looked for hot pink. There were blobs of it here and there, but none were Gigi.

"I hope they didn't drown," she said.

He snorted impatiently. "Why don't you try not being neurotic for a whole hour?"

"I'll try." Suddenly she spotted him and began to run, struggling clumsily through the sand. "Drewie?"

He was a block away. Gigi was sitting on another flight of steps with a dark-haired young man. Drew hopped about, picking things up and digging. He flung a handful of sand into the air. Gigi reached out to stop him.

Debra tried to run faster. Gigi could be harsh with him at times. Her expectations were too rigorous, considering his age.

Gigi greeted Debra with a brilliant smile, dimpling prettily. "Oh, hi."

She did not get up from the steps, but her companion did. He was an extremely handsome youth, wearing a white T-shirt and cut-off jeans. Both he and Gigi were barefooted, their shoes beside them on the steps.

Gigi introduced him. "This is Todd Jorgenson. He lives on the next block from us. This is my stepmother Debra and my dad."

Kurt had arrived just behind Debra. "Todd," he said, and reached over to shake the young man's hand.

"Nice to meet you, sir," Todd replied. Such impeccable manners. Gigi glowed with pleasure.

"Come on, Drewie," Debra said. "It's almost time for your supper. And you didn't have a nap today."

"Wanna stay." Drew pulled away from her.

"He slept in the car," Gigi reminded her.

"That's not a real nap. I want him to get to bed early."

"Early!" exclaimed Gigi. "It's still afternoon. I'm glad I'm not a little kid. Dad, can we eat out?"

"I guess we'll have to," said Kurt, and glanced uneasily at Drew, whose behavior in public places was unpredictable.

"Even McDonald's would be okay," said Gigi, knowing what the glance meant. "Is there a McDonald's?" she asked Todd.

"There's a Burger King," he said, "and Roy Rogers, and some pizzerias, and a place that delivers Chinese food. You can eat there, too."

"Oh, yes, Chinese food! Where is it?"

He gave her directions to the Szechuan Jade. They would have to go there to pick up the food, since their telephone was not yet connected.

"But Drew can't eat Chinese food," Debra protested.

"Why not?" asked Gigi. "He doesn't have to use chopsticks. Like Chinese kids do," she added, implying that Drew was inferior.

Debra grew defensive. "He's not used to it, that's all. He's had enough strangeness for one day."

"We can get him a hamburger," said Kurt. "Are we ready for dinner? I guess I am."

"I'll see you back at the house," Gigi told them. "In a while."

"There isn't going to be any while," her father replied. "We're all going out and we're going to lock the door."

"You won't wait for me? Okay, then I'll sit outside." Gigi smiled at the young man.

Kurt took Debra's elbow and led her up the steps. "Let's try this other street for a change of scene."

Debra looked back at Gigi and her friend, the blond head and the dark one. "And you say I spoil Drew."

"That's not spoiling," said Kurt. "If she wants to sit outside, it's up to her."

"But we don't know anything about that boy."

"Why, did he look sinister to you?"

"Kurt! You can't go by looks."

"Listen, Gigi makes friends at school that her mother and I don't know. It's just part of life."

At the mention of Gigi's mother, Debra was silenced. Their marriage had ended in divorce, but she couldn't get over the idea that Nancy had known him first and perhaps better. Certainly, by this time, longer.

She never knew why they had divorced. After she found out about Kurt's involvement with another woman, she wondered if it might have been something like that.

She herself had not considered divorce. She only ignored what went on, tried to pretend it wasn't happening, and hoped he would get over it.

Drew began to whimper. She picked him up and carried him. They emerged from the park onto a street of small, neat houses crowded together because it was prime shore area. There were picket fences, picturesque gates, rosebushes, and feathery mimosa treees. There was an odor of barbecuing steaks.

"Compared with these, we have quite a palace, haven't we?" said Kurt.

"Yes, we have." She sounded uncertain.

"What's wrong now?"

"I don't know. It's just . . . Well, there's something about that house. It bothers me."

"What do you mean? What's wrong?"

"I'm not sure. But it bothered Drew, too. If I didn't feel it myself, I'd think it was just that he's not used to it."

"Oh, great. Do you mean I have two neurotics on my hands? A big one and a little one?"

"Maybe some people are just more sensitive than others," she answered stiffly. "Maybe we can sense . . . Well, you know that some things leave an imprint."

"I don't know anything of the kind. It's a lot of baloney."

"It's true, Kurt. Maybe you know your Chaucer, but you don't know everything."

"Debra, darling—"

She didn't listen. She was trying to feel what she had felt before. Was it an imprint from the suicide?

Or was it more a sense of something still to come?

Maybe he was right, and she was neurotic after all.

CHAPTER 4

"So you didn't like him," said Lois as they sat in Enid's garden, drinking iced tea.

"Not really," Enid replied. "I don't think it's what I'm looking for."

"I guess I don't understand what you're looking for. I mean realistically."

"What's so unrealistic? All I want is somebody with a little warmth, who can act as if he cares. I wanted to feel better, but he only made it worse."

Eagerly, Lois asked, "What did he say?"

Receiving no answer, she added, "You know, they have support groups for people like you."

"I know. Parents of Suicides. But I don't want to go and listen to all those stories."

"Well," said Lois, "you listen to yourself all the time."

"Thanks. Maybe I should try it. I might get more understanding from a place like that than I get from any of you," Enid told her.

"I try to be understanding."

"Is that what you're doing when you tell me Billy shot himself because I, quote, spoiled him?"

"Honey, I was trying to help you," Lois protested.

"How does that help? Tell me."

"Well, if I told you before—you know, before the accident—you wouldn't have listened."

Enid conceded that she probably would not have. "Anyway, how do you know you're right?" she asked. "What makes you think you're right and I'm wrong?"

Lois stared into her tea glass. "Well . . ."

Her inflection told the story. She was obviously right and Enid wrong because Billy had obviously shot himself, hadn't he?

"I still think it's pointless," Enid said. "I could use a little moral support instead of all this criticism right now. But you're not the only one. It must make everybody feel very superior to see how badly I failed."

"Enid!"

"I'm sorry. I suppose you tried, in your way, but you just don't understand. How would you like it if it happened to you? How would you like to go down in the basement and find Vicky there—"

"Stop it!" cried Lois. "Don't wish that on Vicky."

"I'm not wishing. I just want you to know what it's like. And imagine that going on forever. No more happy, lively Vicky again, ever."

Lois stood up. "I think it's time for me to go."

Enid stood, too, triumphant. "You see? That's what I live with. And you can't even think about it happening to you. Then how would you like it if everybody told you Vicky did it because you failed her?"

Lois's face had gone white. But the anguish was for herself, Enid knew, because she was being tormented.

Lois called her daughters, and then spoke hurriedly to Enid. "Please understand. Billy's my nephew. I always loved him, too."

"That's not what I'm talking about," said Enid. "But thanks for trying. I know you meant well."

She watched the car drive away and felt that she had scored something, but was not sure what. It really hadn't helped. Nothing helped, and nothing ever would.

She was washing the tea glasses when someone knocked on her screen door. She looked through the window to see Todd Jorgenson. He had a girl with him, a pretty blonde.

It wasn't fair. Todd, who had more or less grown up with Billy, was whole and healthy and free to live his life as a young man should. He would have a career and someday marry. Hazel Jorgenson would get a chance to be a grandmother.

She managed to swallow her resentment as she opened the door.

Todd smiled politely and a little apologetically.

"Evening, Mrs. Maul. You wouldn't happen to have a key to that house, would you?"

"Why?" asked Enid.

"Because this girl lives there now. This is Gigi Gillis." He grinned at the girl. "Her folks went off to dinner and locked her out."

The girl smiled charmingly. "It's nice to meet you, Mrs. Maul."

"Well, okay," said Enid. "I'll open the door for you, but the key stays in my possession."

They followed her over to the other house.

"Your parents were right to lock up, with all the burglaries," she told the girl, "but you'd better get yourself a key. Tell your dad to make you a copy. And, Todd, I think you should go home."

He flashed her a smile. "Right, Mrs. Maul."

When the two were inside, she heard the girl say, "You really should. They could be here anytime, and I don't want to get—"

Enid started back up the driveway. She had done her part. If they got into trouble, it was not her problem.

The encounter made her lonelier than ever. Those Gillises were a family. Todd and the girl were a couple.

She had just entered the house when Frank came home. He stood in the doorway, mopping his face.

"You look nice, Enid."

"Thank you," she said, and began to set the table. Frank went to the bedroom to change.

He was a big man, and dark. His hair was deep brown and so were his eyes. Even when freshly shaven he had a shadow on his face, and that made him darker still.

He had been handsome once, in a brooding way. Now his face was heavier. To a stranger, he might have looked tough. That would have been misleading, for he was really not so hardboiled. He had cried after Billy shot himself, but only once and very briefly. Then he went on with his life. It was something Enid had not been able to do.

They ate a dinner of potato salad and cold meat. Frank had put on a blue T-shirt and his hair was still damp from a splashing with cool water. In some ways he reminded her of Billy. Maybe it was the wet hair, which made him appear younger.

"How did it go?" he asked.

She looked up from her salad. "How did what go?"

"The new people."

"Oh, I guess they're okay. I met the wife and the daughter. She's already gotten to know Todd. They were making cow eyes at each other."

"Sheep's eyes," he corrected her.

"What difference?"

"I assume you mean the daughter, not the wife. Is she pretty?"

"Who?"

"The daughter," he said impatiently, "if Todd's already fallen for her."

"Cute. Blond." Her throat tightened. It should have been Billy with a girl like that. But then they would not have had to rent the house and there wouldn't have been any girl. It was only because they needed the money.

"What's the wife like?" he asked.

"Why do you want to know?"

"They're our tenants. I couldn't ask the husband what his wife was like. Besides, I'm doing my best to make conversation."

"Dark hair," said Enid, trying to remember more exactly. "Nice, I guess. Maybe a little . . . I don't know. Self-effacing. Anxious to please. She has a little kid."

"Yes, I know. He told me when he took the place. Boy or girl?"

"What difference?"

Frank shrugged. "None, I guess. I was thinking of the house. A boy might be more apt to tear up the place."

"Then you just charge them for damage."

"That's what I'll have to do. What are you dressed up for, Enid? Shopping? Visiting?"

"Visiting," she said after a moment. She didn't want to tell him about Dr. Longwort.

"But why the fancy duds?"

"It makes me feel better."

He gave her a stiff smile. "I'm glad something does."

She wished she hadn't said that. It wasn't true.

"How are things going?" he asked.

"About the same."

"No change?"

"A little. Maybe."

After dinner Frank announced that he was going out to buy beer. He still had two cans in the refrigerator, so she knew that was not the real reason.

"Why didn't you pick it up on your way?" she asked.

"How did I know we were almost out of it?"

"All right, Frank. Whatever." There was no sense in discussing it and listening to his excuses.

He had scarcely left when there was another knock at the door. This was getting to be too much. If those Gillises didn't stop bothering her—

It was Hazel Jorgenson, a tall, rangy woman with dark hair tied back in a ponytail. She wore a bright pink Mexican shirt.

"Hi, Enid, how are you doing?"

"I'm okay," Enid said wearily. The thought of company made her tired.

"I just wondered if you happened to see Todd anywhere." Hazel looked around the kitchen and peered into the living room. "This is cute."

"Haven't you been here before?"

"No, you always had tenants in this house. How are you doing, Enid?"

"You asked me that already. I'm okay."

Hazel wandered over to the dinette table and rested her hand on the back of the chair. She wanted to stay and talk.

"I saw Todd a little while ago," Enid said. "He was with the girl who moved in over there."

"Oh, that Todd!" exclaimed Hazel. "All he has to do is see a pretty girl and he's off like a—"

At Enid's cold stare, the boasting stopped.

Sobered, Hazel asked, "Where's Frank? Didn't he come home yet?"

"He went out to buy beer."

And of course Hazel thought she believed that.

"What are they like? Your new tenants." Hazel pulled out the chair and sat down.

Reluctantly Enid joined her.

"College professor," she said. "Wife. Couple of kids."

"Are they our age?"

"Young. At least she is. He's youngish."

"I usually think of professors as old."

"Nobody's born old," Enid said irritably. She wondered if Frank would make a play for the wife.

He told me I looked nice, she thought. I didn't even ask him. He just said it.

"Did you see the doctor today?" asked Hazel.

Enid jumped. "What doctor?"

"Lois told me you were going to see a psychologist."

"That's the first I heard of it." Enid promised herself that Lois would die for this.

"Well, okay. It's not my business. You know, Enid, we used to be such pals."

"Really."

"Don't you remember? We used to be able to talk. I know what it's been like for you, but you can't keep this up forever."

"I appreciate your advice, Hazel."

"I mean it. Do you think Billy would want you moping around?"

Enid shrugged. "He might. Who knows? What's the point in destroying yourself, if not to make people sorry?"

Hazel stared at her. "That's a funny way to talk."

"Very funny."

"But maybe you're right." Hazel nodded, her eyes widening thoughtfully.

"You know, maybe you're right," she said again. "Maybe this is good for you. You're starting to get some perspective."

"Hazel, I really don't need somebody to tell me my feelings."

"No, but I mean it. You were always too involved with Billy, do you know that? I'm a firm believer in letting kids grow by themselves."

Enid said nothing. It was her own belief that Hazel had not been involved enough with Todd, except to stand over him and crack the whip while he did his homework.

"It wasn't easy for me," Hazel went on, "having to do it alone."

"We all have our self-pities," Enid murmured.

"But I let Todd know he wasn't going to run my life. *I* was going to run my life, and he could just learn to accommodate me. It's not good for a kid to think the sun rises because of him."

"Isn't there a happy medium?"

"I don't know if there's a happy medium. I just did what I had to do. Remember, I didn't have a husband to back me up."

"Good for you, Hazel. You're one tough cookie."

"You bet I am. And it paid off. It really did."

Enid gripped the table. "You all thought I was too soft on Billy, right? You thought I let him get away with everything."

Hazel relented. "Maybe not *everything*."

"Well, you might be interested to know that just that morning I told him if he didn't stop collecting tickets I was going to take away his car. It wasn't in his name, you know. We could have taken it. He got mad and we had a big row, and then I had to go to work, and when I came home . . . Well,

Hazel, how do you think I like having to live with that?"

She had never told anyone before.

"Oh, Enid." Hazel got up and went to put her hand on Enid's shoulder.

Enid stiffened. Then she began to cry. "So I got tough with him, I cracked down, and look what happened."

"Oh, but, honey, don't you see? You took him by surprise. He wasn't used to it. You should have done it all along, like I did."

"But I loved him."

"That's not love," Hazel said. "It's not love if you let them get away with murder."

"I know that. But it was hard with Frank being the way he is. Anyhow, don't you dare tell me I didn't love my kid."

"Of course you did." Hazel gave the shoulder a squeeze. "I'd better go and see if I can round mine up somewhere. Do you think he's over there?" She nodded toward the Gillis home.

"I heard the girl telling him to leave," said Enid.

She had not meant it as a dig, but it seemed to be taken as one. With studied innocence, Hazel announced, "I was going to pick up some things at the store, but Frank's taking so long to get his beer, I figure there must be a terrible line."

Enid answered calmly, "I wouldn't be surprised. All the summer people."

"It's not really summer yet," Hazel pointed out. "It's still June."

"Right as usual. Maybe Todd's at home now, waiting for you."

"Todd? Wait for me?" Hazel laughed. "He leads his life and I lead mine. We understand each other. I'll see you, dear. Take care."

She was gone. At last. Enid felt drained, as she always did after a cry. She went to the living room and turned on the television.

Upstairs in her old house she saw a lighted window. Someone was moving back and forth across it.

Then something round appeared at the lower part of the window. A small head. The larger figure picked up the smaller one and carried it away.

Enid clenched her jaw. It was just her luck that they had put their child on that side of the house, where she would have to see it and hear it.

She had told Frank she didn't want a family with children. He maintained that it would be nearly impossible to rent a house that size to just a couple. And Frank was in the business. He knew.

But Enid knew herself. She knew how it was going to be, and this was only the first day.

CHAPTER 5

On Tuesday, Kurt prepared for a day of meetings, conferences, and orientation at the college.

"Don't forget," he told Debra, "the reception's at five. I'll come and pick you up."

"Is it only for couples, or for families?" she asked.

"What do you mean by families?"

"I was wondering about Drew and Gigi."

"Absolutely not." He slapped the edge of the table, startling Drew, who was making a mess with an English muffin. "You're not bringing any two-year-old to a faculty party. What are you trying to do?"

"Nothing," she said. "But I hate leaving him alone. We don't know anybody here. We don't know what sort of place this is . . ."

"Debra, you're out of your mind. To begin with, he won't be alone. Second, if you keep this up, you'll make him as neurotic as you are. Is that what you want?"

"No," she said, near tears. "But we only came here yester-

43

day. It's too soon to go off and leave him."

"What's the difference?" roared Kurt. "We're not abandoning him if we leave him with Gigi."

"Quiet, she'll hear you." Debra looked toward the door that led to Gigi's room.

"What are you afraid of, that she'll find out you don't think she's competent?"

"I just don't want to wake her."

But Kurt had won that round. He made perfect sense—to himself. How could she explain her fears about an unknown town? About a wide-open house with front and back doors and numerous ground-level windows? By comparison, their former apartment seemed a bastion.

How could she explain her opinion that Gigi was flighty and self-centered? What was to prevent her from being lured away by that hunk down the street?

She took a deep, resigned breath and asked in a watery voice, "What shall I wear?"

"A nice dress," said Kurt. "A party dress. It's sort of a cocktail party. Wear something suitable but not overly sexy."

"Oh, Kurt, all my dresses are so daring." She tried for humor, but she felt like crying.

He saw through it. "You're just homesick," he said. "Wait till you meet some of these people and settle in. Then you'll be fine."

He was treating her like a child. She supposed she deserved it. He gave her a quick kiss, patted Drew on the head, and left. Debra heard him whistling as he unlocked the car.

He had a good life. She wondered if hers was perhaps too narrow. Maybe that was why she worried so much. As she washed the dishes, she tried to imagine going out and taking a job.

It was no use. She could never leave Drew with anyone else.

Nor would she want to spend her days anywhere but in his company.

Gigi came into the kitchen wearing a pink shortie nightgown that barely brushed the top of her thighs. Debra was relieved to see that it included a pair of lace-edged panties. Gigi's hair was tousled and her face still puffy with sleep.

"Dad leave already?" she asked through a yawn.

"A few minutes ago," said Debra.

Another yawn. "I might be going to the beach with Todd."

"How come Todd isn't working this summer?"

Gigi bristled. "He couldn't find a job. He's still looking."

"Couldn't he be a lifeguard?"

"Debra, those jobs are gone by February. The best ones always go early. He just missed out, that's all." Gigi drank a glass of orange juice, then went to take a shower and get ready for Todd.

She was still in the bathroom when he arrived half an hour later. Debra let him in and went back to the living room, where she was unpacking cartons of books and records. Drew played on the floor beside her with a fleet of toy cars.

Todd flipped through the scattered albums. "You've got some nice things here. Great classical stuff."

"We have folk music, too," Debra said. "My husband likes that. And the Beatles. A little vintage rock."

"How come you're not at the beach today?"

She smiled. At his age, probably the beach was the only place to be.

"I'm waiting for the phone company," she said. "We'll go over later. Anyway, there's a lot to do right here. If I work at it now and then, it doesn't seem so bad."

"Need any help?"

"Oh, no thanks. It's mostly a matter of putting things away."

"Well, stick around for a while," he suggested. "I think my

mother's coming over to see you. She's making blueberry muffins."

"How nice of her," said Debra. "I'd like to meet your mother."

"Gigi met her yesterday. I took her over there."

"Do you have more family? Brothers or sisters?"

"I have my dad, but he's in Seattle. I see him about every ten years." Todd stopped to watch as Drew rattled an empty bookcase, listening to the vibration of its steel shelves.

Drew tugged harder and the bookcase tipped. Before Debra could get up off the floor, Todd had caught it.

"Oh, my God," Debra gasped. "I don't know how to thank you. Really. He could have been killed." She pulled Drew onto her lap.

"Not killed, maybe, but it would have hurt him." Todd pushed the bookcase into a corner. "Do you want us to take him to the beach? Keep him out of your way?"

"No, I—" Debra's heart still pounded. It had been so close.

"He's not really in the way," she said. "I can't imagine what made me so careless."

Gigi appeared wearing a pair of light blue shorts and a striped blouse. The blouse was unbuttoned, showing an amazing one-piece suit that left her entire midsection bare. She carried a rolled beach towel under her arm.

"I don't know when I'll be back," she said.

"Have fun," Debra told them. "Be careful. Remember, the sun is very strong right now."

She was on her third carton when a man arrived to connect the telephone. As soon as it was done she called Kurt's office to give him the new number. He had left a message, the secretary said, reminding Debra of the reception that afternoon.

"I don't want to go to any stupid old party," she told Drew as she hugged him tightly. "I just want to stay here with you."

He fought his way out of her arms. "Want my *cars!*"

"I know what we can do. You bring your boats and I'll get some water. We can play outside for a while."

She found a plastic dishpan and filled it with water from an outdoor faucet. Drew brought an armful of toys including a submarine and a waterwheel. He dumped them all into the dishpan.

"I think it's better if you play with them one at a time." She began lifting them out of the water. Drew set up a howl.

In the middle of it, a cheery voice called, "Hi, there!"

A lanky, dark-haired woman was coming toward them, carrying a covered tray.

"You're Mrs. Gillis, aren't you?" she said. "I'm Hazel Jorgenson. I understand you've been seeing a lot of my son Todd since you moved in."

"I'm so glad to meet you." Debra took the offered tray. It proved to be a shallow cardboard box lined with aluminum foil. The muffins were still warm. She brewed a pot of coffee and brought out two chairs so they could sit under the oak tree in the yard.

Hazel beamed at Drew. "Isn't he sweet. I'll bet he likes living here, doesn't he?"

"He didn't at first," said Debra, "but I think he's getting used to it. At least he can play outside whenever he wants. We lived in an apartment before."

"I met your other child, Gigi. Your stepdaughter, right? That's what she told me."

"She would have to make that clear." Debra tried to laugh it off. "I'm afraid she doesn't admire me terribly much."

"It's probably a put-on," Hazel said. "Teenagers can be so difficult. I should know."

"Todd's in college, isn't he? At Luna College, where my husband teaches?"

"Yes, he just finished his first year. He's looking for a job. Not much luck so far." Hazel rolled her eyes. "As long as he doesn't hang around the house and drive me crazy. And he hasn't asked for money, so it must be all right."

"That's good, if he can get along."

"He seems to have enough left from high schoool. He used to deliver pizza in the afternoons, and saved quite a lot."

Debra remembered that Hazel was divorced. "Do you work outside the home?"

"I have to," Hazel said. "I teach math at the high school. It's not easy when you're alone, but I manage. And raising a child, too. All these people around here, Enid Maul, they all have husbands."

"Yes, it does help," Debra agreed. "It must be hard trying to do it by yourself."

"It's not easy, I'll say that. But I get by."

"From what I've seen of Todd, you did very well with him. He seems like a nice young man. How old is he now?"

"He's nineteen."

"Gigi's only fifteen."

"Really?" That seemed to amuse Hazel. "I thought she was older. So mature and self-assured. Actually, I only saw her for a few minutes. They do make a handsome pair, don't they?"

"Yes, they do."

But he was so much older, Debra thought. Was it really all right? It was up to Kurt to put his foot down, however. Gigi would never listen to Debra.

"Have you met any of the people around here?" Hazel asked. "The Mauls, probably."

"Yes, I met Mrs. Maul. She stopped by just as we were moving in. But I haven't seen the husband yet. Only his car."

Hazel seemed about to speak, but unsure as to whether she ought to. Finally, she said, "You probably won't see him very often. He doesn't spend a lot of time at home. He has—well, other interests."

"What do you mean?"

As soon as she said it, Debra realized what Hazel meant. Her face grew hot.

"Other interests besides his family and work," Hazel said. "*You* know what I mean."

"Yes."

She could not have meant that Debra would know firsthand. She couldn't mean that. How would she have guessed?

Hazel stretched out her legs and studied the bright red espadrilles on her feet.

"Poor Enid. We could all see it coming. I mean it's very sad, after what happened, but she really didn't give much thought to her husband. I think it's some girl who works in the bank."

"Oh."

"It's really awful for her. Everybody knows about it. But you've got to look at his side, too. She was always so involved with Billy, even before . . . you know. Frank probably started feeling left out. Have you been to the beach yet?"

The words echoed. *Frank started feeling left out.*

"No, not yet. We were too busy yesterday. I think Gigi's there now with Todd."

"I hope you have something to put over the baby," Hazel said. "An umbrella, maybe. The sun can be pretty fierce in June."

They were on safer ground.

"Yes, I know." Debra gave in to lively chatter. "I have a terrible time with him. His hair is dark, but look how fair his skin is. I have to make him wear a shirt even when it's hot, and that can be a struggle. At least he has thick enough hair to protect his head, so he doesn't have to wear a cap."

"So adorable at that age." Hazel rose from her chair. "Well, I won't keep you. I know you have things to do."

"It's so nice of you to stop by," Debra told her. "I hope you'll come again. And the muffins were delicious. I'll save the rest for Kurt and Gigi."

She and Drew changed into their swimsuits. They would be able to have a little time at the beach before lunch. She would have preferred to go later in the day when the sun was lower, but there was that tiresome party.

What if Gigi didn't come back in time? Debra almost hoped she wouldn't. Then Kurt would understand how irresponsible she was.

Drew was familiar with the ocean from having lived on Long Island. He enjoyed digging in the sand and collecting shells. He liked holding his mother's hand as they jumped in the foam that washed ashore.

After an hour she took him home and fed him lunch. While he napped, she washed and dried her hair. She picked out a dress, a blue one that Kurt liked, with a swirling skirt and a V neckline that was not too low. She had bought it for a party at his former school, and had had a pair of shoes dyed to match. She hoped it was not too dressy. If only she knew some of the other women, she could have asked what they were wearing.

In the middle of the afternoon, Kurt called to say he would see her at four-thirty and hoped she would be ready.

"I will," she said. "But Gigi's not home yet. She went to the beach this morning with Todd and she hasn't come back."

"She'll be there," Kurt assured her.

Debra watched the clock. With every minute that went by, her hopes rose. Maybe Kurt would have to go to the party alone.

He would be furious. But it was not her fault.

By four-twenty, she was dressed and ready to leave. Gigi had still not appeared.

Kurt would say she had not really tried. But she didn't know anybody, except perhaps Hazel Jorgenson. She looked for the name in the telephone book. There were three Jorgensons, including a "Mrs. S." on Angel Road. She tried calling, but no one answered.

Taking Drew with her, she went over to the Maul house. When Enid finally answered the door, she seemed harried. Debra had caught her in the middle of dressing to go out.

"Is something wrong?" Enid asked.

"I'm sorry to bother you," said Debra. "I was supposed to go to a party at the college this afternoon. My husband's very insistent. I thought my stepdaughter would be home to babysit, but she hasn't come back. I wonder . . . Do you know of anyone I could trust?"

"A baby sitter? No, I don't. I really don't know anybody."

"I just wondered . . . since you've been here a while." Debra grasped at the door that was starting to close. "Do you think your sister would know anybody?"

"I couldn't say. But she's not home."

"Well . . . thank you." Debra turned away, concealing her elation. She owed Enid a vote of thanks.

Her pleasure was short-lived. Gigi had come home and was in the kitchen, drinking orange juice.

"I'm here." Gigi smiled blandly. She seemed dazed, as though she had had too much sun.

"You had me worried," Debra lied. "I went over to ask Mrs. Maul if she knew any sitters."

"Why, did you think I wouldn't make it?"

"Your dad's coming any minute to pick me up."

"Well, I'm here." Gigi set down her glass and drifted toward her room.

"Are you all right?" Debra asked.

"Why shouldn't I be all right? All I have to do is take a shower."

"You seem a little . . . I don't know."

"I'm fine!" Gigi snapped. A moment later, the shower was running.

Kurt drove in and bounded up the back steps.

"Gigi just came home," Debra said.

"I told you she'd be here," he crowed.

"I'm not leaving till she's out of the shower."

They waited ten minutes. Gigi emerged wearing a clean shirt of her father's, a towel around her hair, and very little else.

"What's the problem?" she demanded when she saw them still there.

"No problem," said Kurt. "We're off."

"Have fun," Gigi told them grumpily as they went out to the car.

Debra thought she still did not seem quite normal, but Kurt was unworried.

"What does she have to do?" he asked. "Just give the kid his supper, right?"

"And maybe put him to bed. And . . ." Debra did not know how to explain. Drew needed someone who cared.

"We'll be back long before he has to go to bed," said Kurt. "They'll be okay. You look smashing, by the way."

"Thank you." She had a terrible feeling of unease. As their car turned onto Barton Avenue, she looked back at the house.

"Kurt, I don't know if it was the sun."

"What are you talking about?"

"Gigi. How can anybody get that spaced out just from the sunshine?"

"You can get skin cancer from sunshine. Isn't that worse?" he said.

"I guess so. But she didn't look any more tan. If she was out long enough to fry her brains, you'd think she would have gotten more tan."

"Maybe she had a cover on, okay? What are you suggesting?"

"I don't know. And then sometimes she gets nervous. Sometimes she's very short-tempered with Drew."

"Uh—" He gave an uneasy laugh. "So am I sometimes. But that doesn't mean anybody's going to beat him up, so take it easy, will you?"

She wanted to, but she didn't know how. She tried to forget about Drew and Gigi as they approached the college, a complex of low modern buildings with many windows.

"It's very attractive," she said.

"Not your traditional college architecture," he agreed, "but it's light and airy. I like that."

He parked the car and led her up a paved walk between the library and the science building, to a large, grassy quadrangle. Long tables had been set up to one side of it, and people stood about in clusters, eating, drinking, and chatting.

"See?" said Kurt. "Not a two-year-old in sight. Not one."

She realized that it would have been idiotic to bring Drew. She had supposed he might have been the center of attention, with people fussing over him, but that, she saw, was nonsense. She would simply have made a fool of herself and of Kurt, too.

"I'm sorry," she said.

"All right." He was good-natured about it, but with a bite. "For penance, instead of two hundred pushups, you will relax and enjoy yourself. No more neuroses for the next three hours."

"Are we going to be here three hours?" she asked in alarm.

"Ah!" He held up a finger. "Don't start."

A well-endowed young woman in a décolleté dress came over to greet them. Her face was round and somewhat plain, Debra thought, but surrounded by a magnificent swirl of strawberry blond hair.

"How are you doing, Kurt?" the woman asked. "Is this your missus?"

"Yes, this is Debra," he replied. "Meet Georgia Peach, one of the ladies in our department."

"How do you do . . . Georgia." Debra looked from one to the other.

The woman laughed. "It's really Sharon, but my last name is Pietsch, so Georgia's a natural. I think it's kind of cute."

Kurt and Georgia talked of school matters, while Debra sipped her wine.

She wanted to be at home with Drew. But Kurt had forbidden her even to think of it.

What did he expect her to do? She did not belong here. She had no interest in these people. Especially Georgia Pietsch.

After Georgia left them, Kurt spotted the college president and his wife. He pulled Debra at a fast trot across the grass to meet them.

Next came the department head, and someone emeritus, then a Russian professor and two secretaries.

Debra could not remember names. Only faces. She smiled when she saw the same ones again. But it seemed that everywhere she went with Kurt, they kept running into Georgia Pietsch.

"Small world, isn't it?" Georgia remarked.

"Very," said Debra. "Have you been here long?"

"About five years."

"Are you by yourself?" Debra had looked in vain for a husband or a boyfriend.

"Do you mean, am I married?" Georgia laughed. "I'm mostly divorced. Well, separated, anyway."

"Do you have children?"

"No, thank God for that. I'm not ready to be tied down."

Again Debra sipped her wine. She wanted to cling to Kurt,

but he was too busy meeting new people and politicking.

She was corraled by an elderly woman in a pink dress, who asked what her name was and where she had come from.

"And where are you living now?" was the next question.

"We're on Barton Avenue," Debra said. "We're renting from some people named Maul."

"Oh." The woman's tone became hushed. "The family that had that awful tragedy. He was a student here, you know. That boy."

"No, I didn't know."

"A freshman. His first year. Such a tragedy. What sort of things are you interested in, Mrs. Gillis?"

"Well—mostly I'm a homemaker. I have a young child . . ."

"Yes, but you must have an outside interest. There are a lot of activities here for faculty families as well as students. We have language groups and current events. We have a literature discussion group. You said your husband's in the literature department? Maybe you'd like that."

"I don't really get out very much," Debra said. "My child is only two, and I don't have a car. My husband uses our only car."

"Oh, there must be some arrangements you can make. We have action groups, too. There are the anti-nuke people. There are mothers and students against drunk driving. There's GADOC."

Debra smiled. "That sounds like something out of Tolkien."

"It's Get All Drugs Off Campus," explained the woman. "A very good idea, but I never understood why the rest of us have to form an organization. Why can't people just not take them? It's ridiculous. Well, you're closer to that age than I am. Maybe you understand it better."

"Not really," said Debra. "But I heard it's quite a problem."

"Terrible. Terrible. It seems so stupid. How old did you say your child is? A boy or a girl?"

For the first time, Debra began to enjoy herself as she told the woman about Drew. Then a man joined them and again the literature group was mentioned. Everyone seemed to think she ought to be interested.

"Well, actually," Debra said, "my own field, when I was in college, was archeology, but I—"

"There, you see?" exclaimed the woman. "I knew we'd think of something. Unfortunately there isn't an archeology group at the moment. But that's not to say you couldn't start one." With that, she left to accost someone else.

Debra looked around for Kurt. Finally she saw him under a tree near the refreshment tables.

He was deep in earnest and intimate conversation with a strawberry blonde in a décolleté dress.

Debra turned away and took another gulp of wine, hiding behind her glass.

CHAPTER 6

Half sitting, half lying, Gigi sprawled on the living-room sofa, her long, bare legs stretched out in front of her. She felt at peace.

"Maybe I'll stay here," she said to Todd. "In Luna Beach. I like it better than where I came from."

He sat beside her, gazing up at the ceiling. "Why? What's so good about it?"

"Oh, you know. It has everything I want." She giggled. "I'm feeling good."

"You should be."

She nudged him with her foot. "Don't keep telling me what I should. Don't spoil everything."

"What's to spoil?"

"Everything."

Drew flung himself at her lap. "Wanna see the water."

"No, thanks," Gigi said. "I was there all day. What are you trying to do to me?"

"Why don't you put him in bed so we can go somewhere?" Todd suggested.

"I can't do that. What if they come back and find him alone?"

"Up to you. But I don't want to sit around here all night." He rose to his feet.

She jumped up. "Don't go, Todd. Maybe we could . . . Is there any place we could go where we can take him with us?"

"Are you crazy? I don't know. Maybe up the street. It's nothing exciting, but it's not very far."

"What's there?"

"Something. I'll show you. Ever wonder why it's called Angel Road?"

"Not really," she admitted. "I never thought about it. Where are we going?"

"I told you, it's just up the street."

"Come on, Drewie." She held out her hand. "Do we have to lock the house?"

"No, that's dumb," said Todd. "If they're going to break in, they'll do it anyway."

"See the water!" Drew exclaimed as Gigi helped him down the back steps.

"No, we're not," she said, "and don't bug me about it. We're going the other way."

They climbed over the fence and turned up Angel Road. Drew pulled on her arm.

"Wanna see the *water*," he wailed, and stamped both his feet.

Gigi said, "I'm warning you."

"Want me to give him something?" asked Todd.

"Oh, God, no." She laughed until she sagged against a telephone pole. "They'd kill me. They'd ship me back home in a box. It's just that this kid is so spoiled. All he has to do is start hollering and Debra gives him anything he wants."

"How would they know?" Todd took Drew's other arm and they marched him forward up the street. Immediately he chortled, lifted his feet, and allowed himself to be swung along between them.

"They'd know," said Gigi. "They know about those things. Dad's real cool, or so he thinks, and Debra's pretty young. They met when she was in one of his classes."

"What happened? She took him away from your mom?"

"No, they were already divorced. What are we going to see?"

"Nothing. Just a grave."

"What grave?"

"A kid. It's more than a hundred years old."

"You mean there's a cemetery near here? Right near where I sleep?"

"No, it's just one grave."

"I thought people had to be buried in cemeteries."

"Maybe they don't," he said. "I don't know. I wasn't around then. Maybe there was some reason."

"Like what?"

"Like maybe he could have done it himself."

"Buried himself?"

"No. Killed himself."

"Like Billy Maul?"

Todd glanced at her and turned away. She remembered that Billy had been his friend.

"It used to be," he said, "that they couldn't put them in hollow . . . hallowed ground. I don't know about now."

"I do. A kid I knew committed suicide and he got buried in a cemetery."

"That's nice," said Todd.

They passed his house and saw his mother's car in the driveway.

He glowered at it. "I hate summer. She's always around."

"Why, does she bother you?"

"Not so much anymore," he admitted. "She used to give me a real pain. Except all she cared about was my homework. If I didn't do good work, she thought it might make her look bad as a teacher."

"So you did real well in school?"

"Not after I caught on. Then I got involved with other things."

"What other things?"

He did not reply. Gigi stopped short, making Drew kick with annoyance.

"Todd, you're not dealing, are you?"

"What, are you crazy?"

"I just wanted to be sure. A kid at my school got caught selling coke. They threw him out of school and now he has to face charges."

"Getting thrown out of school wouldn't be so bad," Todd said with a laugh. "All you'd have to do is not tell your folks, and then you could sit around all day. Which is what I do anyway."

"Wouldn't they find out?"

"Not necessarily. Not in college. Unless they start to wonder why the bills aren't coming in."

As they crossed the street to the next block, she saw a cluster of trees between the houses.

"Is it there?"

"Right in there," he said. "It's a little place that's fenced off. Nobody can buy or sell that piece of land."

A metal rail separated the plot from the sidewalk. The rail continued around all four sides of a small grassy area, almost a miniature park. A weeping willow tree shaded the grave. The ground around it was littered with beer cans and cigarette butts.

She strained to see what was written on the headstone. It looked very old.

"Come on in." Todd stepped over the rail. She lifted Drew over it and followed.

The inscription was worn and defaced by graffiti. She could barely make out the words.

HERE LIES
AN ANGEL
WILLIAM COTSWORTH
DARNLEY
1844–1847

"William!" she exclaimed, thinking again of Billy Maul. "Who was he?"

"Just some kid, I guess," said Todd.

"He must have been pretty rich if he has this place all to himself and they still keep it up."

Todd rubbed the stone with his sneakered toe. "How do you know he has it all to himself? Maybe there are more people buried here. More little angels."

"There aren't any other markers."

"You don't need markers. It's just a convention. There's no law about it, as far as I know."

"Well," she said, "if the others don't have markers, how come this one does? If there are others."

He grinned. "Want to find out? I could get a shovel."

"No!" she screamed. "They . . . they'd see us."

"Who, the dead people?"

"No, dummy, the people across the street. All the cars. And anyway . . ."

"Cars can't see."

"You know what I mean." She was growing irritated.

He laughed. "You're funny when you're mad."

"I'm not mad. And anyway, I don't want to see a dead body."

"Neither do I," he admitted. "I just wanted to show you this because it's sort of local history. I mean, not real history, but you know."

"Yes, it's very interesting. It really is. Drewie, don't climb on there." She pulled him away from the stone.

"Does he talk much?" asked Todd. "Does he understand things?"

"Some. He understands better than he talks, but he usually won't listen. That's because she spoils him."

"How old is he?"

"Two and a half."

Todd looked thoughtful. "He's got six months to go."

"Before what?"

"Before he's three. Like the dead kid there."

"Three?" She looked at the dates again. "Todd, you dummy, a three-year-old can't commit suicide."

"Who said he did?"

"You did, when we were coming here. You said he might have."

Todd gave her an odd smile. "How do you know they can't?"

"Well, they . . . wouldn't know how. They wouldn't even know to do it. I don't think they know what death is."

"A lot of kids kill themselves," he said. "You read about it all the time."

"Maybe you do, but I don't. Why are you so gruesome? Is it because of Billy Maul?"

"I don't know. Maybe."

"Was he really a good buddy of yours?"

"One of the best."

"I'm sorry."

"Not your fault. He did it to himself."

"Yes, but anyway . . ." She shuddered. "Let's get out of here before it's dark."

"It won't get dark for hours," said Todd. "The sun's still up."

"Yes, but it's darkish here already. Because of the trees, I guess. Anyway, I'd better get Drew home. If they come back and he's not there, Debra's going to have a stroke. She'll call the National Guard. I'll get court-martialed."

Todd laughed. "Sounds like Billy's mom. She was always carrying on. Mine, too, sometimes."

"That's because you're an only child," Gigi said, "and so was he. So's Drew."

"What about you?"

"No, I mean the mother's only child. Debra doesn't care about me."

"On your mother's side?"

"There's three of us, but that wasn't for a long time. Ten years, I guess. Anyhow, my mom always figured I could take care of myself."

"You can? Are you sure?" He eyed her skeptically and again they laughed.

When they reached Todd's house he said goodbye, and she and Drew went on alone.

"Wanna see the water," said Drew.

"Oh, quiet. Didn't we have a nice time? Don't you like Todd? I think he's cool."

"Where's my mommy?"

"She went to a party. So did Dad, but they'll be home soon. It's good for you if they go out. Good for your mom, too. She doesn't think you can exist without her. Or maybe it's the other way."

Mrs. Maul was outside in her garden, trimming the flowers.

Gigi called, "Hello, how are you?"

Impulsively she turned in at the open gate. There were roses all over the gate and fence. A quaint brick walk led up through the garden.

Gigi looked about in admiration. "I just wanted to tell you how much we like the house. It's really nice. And this one's cute, too. You have beautiful flowers."

"I planted them last spring," said Mrs. Maul, "when I knew we were moving in here."

She wore denim shorts and had surprisingly good legs.

"Well, it's gorgeous," Gigi said. "Would it be all right if I planted some things over at our place? I love flowers."

"Sure, if you want. There are a lot of perennials already there, but you can plant anything you like. It's kind of late in the season, though."

"Maybe I can get some ready-made stuff, like pansies. You can get those already blooming."

"You can get a lot of things already blooming," said Mrs. Maul. "Petunias, celosia, marigolds . . ."

Gigi smiled. "I don't know what some of those are, but I'll learn."

She had been curious about the woman, to see what frame of mind she might be in after the terrible thing that had happened. Mrs. Maul seemed quite normal. A lot more relaxed than Debra, who was always fussing over her precious child as if nobody ever had one before.

"Well," said Gigi, "I'd better go on home and put this kid to bed. They went to a party and I have to baby-sit. But I had a nice day at the beach. It's really cool being so close you can walk there. How come you decided to move back to this house, Mrs. Maul?"

As soon as the words were out, she was embarrassed. It probably had something to do with Billy's suicide. Maybe they wanted to forget.

Unperturbed, Mrs. Maul replied, "We needed the money."

"Oh."

"We get a lot more money for renting that house than this one, because it's bigger."

"Oh. Yes," said Gigi. "Well, I think it's cool having two houses on your property. It's almost like an estate."

What did they need the money for? she wondered.

"I never thought of it that way," said Mrs. Maul.

"How come you're trimming the flowers?"

"To take off the dead blossoms. It makes them bloom better. Otherwise they put their energy into making seeds."

"Oh, I never knew that." Gigi picked up one of the fallen stalks and examined it. "I'll bet I could learn a lot from you."

Mrs. Maul actually smiled. "I'm no expert, but don't be afraid to ask. I can always look it up. I have some books."

"That's cool. I'll get my flowers as soon as I can. It's been really nice talking to you. I hope you don't mind if I come over sometime and look at your garden."

"Whenever you want. It'll always be here." Another smile.

I like her, Gigi thought.

She did not know what she had expected. A recluse, perhaps, or someone in deep mourning. Not a perfectly friendly neighbor.

Drew had been fidgeting while she talked. When she turned to leave, he pulled on her arm. "Wanna see the *water*."

"Oh, quiet," she groaned. "You're going to bed, and you'd better not give me any trouble."

She looked back apologetically. "This kid's a spoiled brat," she explained.

Mrs. Maul gave her a bland smile and went on trimming her flowers.

CHAPTER 7

When Kurt and Debra reached home, Gigi was sitting alone in the darkened living room.

"What, no television?" Kurt asked playfully.

"There's nothing on." Gigi sounded quiet and dreamy.

Debra asked, "Are you feeling all right?"

That brought a little more animation. "Why? What's wrong?"

"I just wondered if maybe you got too much sun today at the beach." Debra watched for a reaction.

"I'm okay." Gigi settled back, closing them out.

Debra went upstairs with Kurt. The cushioning fog from her wine had worn off, and she felt merely depressed.

The next morning Gigi slept late and woke in a bad mood. "Did Todd call?" she demanded.

"No, he didn't," said Debra, to which Gigi muttered, "Shit."

"I wish you wouldn't use that word," Debra told her. "I find it very offensive."

"Everybody says it," Gigi snapped, and closed herself in the bathroom.

After a lengthy shower and a glass of orange juice, she seemed to feel better. She went so far as to ask how the party had been.

"Just fine," said Debra. Even to herself she did not sound convincing. "I met a lot of nice people. How was your evening?"

"Okay. Todd was here for a while."

"That's nice." Debra hoped it was nice. She hoped they had both been good with Drew.

"We went for a walk," Gigi said. "And I stopped in to see Mrs. Maul. She has a beautiful garden."

"Yes, I've noticed it. I'm glad she has something pleasant."

"I want to get some flowers. She said she'd help me if I have any questions."

"I'm surprised she's that friendly. She didn't seem very friendly when she came by here on Monday."

"Why?" Gigi asked. "What was wrong with her?"

"I'm not sure, exactly. She wasn't *un*friendly, but—"

She had barely even looked at Drew. No one could ignore a little child. It had seemed deliberate.

Gigi set her orange juice glass in the sink.

"I found out why this is called Angel Road. Todd showed me."

"Why is it?" Debra asked.

"You really have to see it, but I'll tell you. It's a couple of blocks up that way, past Todd's house. There's this place that has a railing around it, and some trees. And there's a grave that says 'Here Lies an Angel.' It's some little kid who died more than a hundred years ago. William something. He was three years old."

"I see."

"It must have been there before all these houses were built," Gigi continued, "but nobody can buy or sell that piece of land. It's still kept up, though. Except for the beer cans. I guess it was there before anything else on the street, so they named it after it."

"Probably. That's interesting."

And sad, Debra thought. Someone must have loved that child very much, to have set up such an elaborate arrangement at a time when young children were as likely to die as not.

Gigi said, "I kept wondering why it was separate like that. People are usually buried in cemeteries, aren't they?" She giggled. "Todd even thought maybe the kid committed suicide. You know, so he couldn't be buried in a regular place. Can you imagine? A three-year-old?"

"No, I can't imagine," Debra said shortly. "You know, a lot of times people used to have their own private graves on their estates. Maybe that family owned all the land around here."

Gigi seemed impressed. "I didn't know you could do that. Have your own grave."

"I'm not sure you can anymore. There are all sorts of laws that regulate those things." Debra opened the bread drawer to make sandwiches to take to the beach.

Gigi asked, "How would they know? If you had a lot of land, how would they know if you buried somebody on it?"

"They'd know if somebody died," Debra explained, "because you have to report it. I really don't know if they check up on what you do then. I never ran into that situation."

"Maybe Billy Maul is buried right here. Maybe that's why she loves her garden so much."

Gigi was staring out of the window at Mrs. Maul's cottage. She hadn't been serious, but she was not joking, either.

Fanciful. That was a good description, Debra thought.

Gigi turned to her, smiling. "Todd's so weird. You know what he said? He asked me how old Drew was, and then he said, 'He's got six months to go.' I asked him what he meant, and he said, 'Before he's three years old like the dead kid there.' Isn't that weird?"

"It's macabre," said Debra.

Gigi grinned. "I didn't think you'd like it much."

Debra took Drew upstairs and readied him for the beach. She felt a lump of unease. It was odd the way Gigi would turn on her in the midst of what had seemed a friendly conversation. It had not been necessary to report what Todd said, even if he really said it. More likely Gigi had made it up to torment her.

The hurt was forgotten during a long and peaceful afternoon at the beach. She was alone with Drew, who was almost part of herself. With him she had no serious conflicts, no real unpleasantness. The only difficulty came when she tried to cover him to prevent a sunburn.

By bribing him with a cookie, she managed to get a shirt over his head and put sunblock cream on his face and legs. She had brought a folding screen that was meant to be a windbreak, but she made it into a cave and he played happily inside it. He took his nap inside it, too, while she drowsed next to him in its shade.

At four o'clock they started home. She was eager to learn how Kurt's day had gone, but dreading that he might have too much to say about Georgia Pietsch.

Kurt was not in the house, nor was Gigi. Probably Gigi was at the beach with Todd. Probably she was lying there in her skimpy bathing suit, glistening with baby oil.

But that was Kurt's problem. He was the only one who could handle it.

Debra was damp from the shower and wearing a pink terrycloth shift when Kurt came home. She knew she smelled nice as he embraced her. Short tendrils of hair curled about her ears and sparkled with stray beads of water.

"You feel warm," he said.

"I took Drew to the beach. I hope I didn't get him burned. How did everything go?"

"Pretty good," he said. "I think it'll be a good year. Classes start next Monday. Here, I brought you something."

It was on the kitchen counter, wrapped in white paper. She knew by the shape that it was flowers. He handed it to her with a mock bow.

"For me?" she asked.

"Who else? What do you think I have, a harem?" He laughed.

She opened the package. It was a dainty bouquet of pink carnations and baby's breath.

"Kurt, how nice! What inspired this?"

"Just one of those things." His smile was soft. She kissed him and clung to him, the flowers still in her hand. Drew clambered about his father's leg and Kurt scarcely noticed.

Suddenly he pulled away, patting his jacket. "What did I do with my keys? Don't tell me I left them in the car."

"How could you, with that horrible noise it makes?" Debra opened the cupboard and searched for a container for the flowers.

A moment later he was back, grinning sheepishly. "Found them. In my pocket."

"Really, you're the proverbial absent-minded professor," she said. "It must have been a grueling day."

"All days are grueling." He laughed again. "Where's Gigi?"

"I don't know. She's been seeing a lot of that Jorgenson boy. I kind of wish he'd get a job and settle down. He's nineteen, you know."

She had meant it as a warning. A subtle snitch. Kurt merely

said, "Uh-huh," and removed his tie.

"Supper in half an hour," she told him as he went upstairs to change his clothes.

She set the table and thought about his odd behavior. He was silly and absent-minded. She wondered if it had anything to do with the Pietsch woman.

Or his old flame Stacie. Or perhaps someone else.

But he had brought flowers and acted very sweet. It couldn't be any of those.

She looked across the yard at the Maul cottage. How odd that the same thing should be going on right next door. Another man like Kurt.

Another woman like Debra.

But Enid Maul was not at all like Debra. Not really. She might have had a cheating husband, but worse than that, she had lost the thing no woman should ever lose. Her child.

It's not going to happen to me, Debra thought.

She and Drew had too close a rapport. She could not imagine any mother being so out of touch with her child that he would feel desolate enough to take his own life. It was obvious that Enid, for whatever reason, must have fallen down on the job.

CHAPTER 8

Enid liked the roses best. Roses had a romance, a mystique. They came in almost every imaginable color and they bloomed all summer, late into the fall. Her lavender ones were opening now. It was a humid day and not too sunny, and their petals still sparkled with morning dew.

A soft voice said, "Hi, Mrs. Maul."

Gigi Gillis was coming up the driveway with a tray of bright pink flowers. She carried it as though she did not know what to do with it.

"Todd took me shopping," she announced. "I got some pansies and other stuff. I forgot what these are."

"Impatiens," said Enid.

"They're real pretty. They had all different shades of pink and orange, and some white, too. I couldn't get them all, but I love it."

"Yes, it's very nice," Enid agreed. "Now stand back a little. I'm dusting the roses and I don't want it to blow in your face."

"I'll get over here." Gigi darted around in back of her. "What is that stuff?"

"It's rose dust. You just puff it out of the bottle."

"Doesn't the rain wash it off?"

"A heavy rain, yes," said Enid. "But I have to do it every so often anyway."

Gigi sat down on a wrought-iron bench with the flowers beside her.

"My dad's already started working over at the school," she said. "He came home all happy and crazy yesterday. I think he found another bimbo."

"A what?" Enid stopped squeezing the bottle, as though its gentle puffing sound might have distorted what she heard.

"A bimbo," Gigi repeated. "Don't you know what that is? He had one where he used to teach, on Long Island. He always does it. That's why my mother decided to split. But Debra never says anything. I don't know if she even knows."

Enid wondered why the girl was telling her this. It seemed a private matter.

Could she know? Enid wondered. About Frank?

How fascinating that the Gillis woman should have the same problem. She, whose life appeared serene and uncomplicated. Who seemed so complacent. When their children were that young, they had no idea what trouble was, or that things could ever change.

"But I don't see how she could help knowing about that last one," Gigi said. "Do you think maybe she just doesn't want to?"

Who are we talking about? Enid wondered. Her or me?

"Could be," she answered cautiously. "A person can know what's happpening but not know how to say anything. Or maybe she's afraid to speak up and have to make a decision."

"About what?"

"About what to do."

"If it was me, I'd just tell him to stop," Gigi declared.

"Yes, but what if he won't? Then what do you do? Maybe she's afraid it would come to that."

"Well, I think it's weak."

"It is," said Enid. "Weak and cowardly. But maybe she knows best what their relationship is like."

Gigi shrugged. "I don't know why she's so scared. She still has Drew. Sometimes I think that's all she cares about anyway."

"Maybe that's what your father thinks, too."

"Huh? Oh, I don't know. She likes my dad okay. But it gets tiresome the way she's always fluttering over Drew and talking about him. I mean, he's Dad's kid, too, but you know. There are other things in the world."

"That's true," said Enid. "That's very true."

"When do you think I should plant my flowers?"

"In the evening, not the heat of the day. And give them plenty of water as soon as they're in the ground."

"I'm glad I asked. See? There's so much I don't know." Gigi laughed softly. "You're one smart lady, Mrs. Maul."

"No," said Enid, "I'm not. That's one thing I'm not. Would you like a Coke? I have some in the refrigerator."

They went into the kitchen, where Enid washed the rose dust from her hands.

"This is a nice place," Gigi said, looking around at the beamed ceiling, the decorative copperware, the Portuguese tiles above the stove and sink. "It's really pretty. I like it."

"Thank you." Enid took a large bottle of Coca-Cola from the refrigerator and poured it into two glasses, which she set at the dinette table. It was cooler in the kitchen than outside.

"I did it over just before we moved in," she explained. "I felt sad about leaving the old house. This was to cheer me up."

Gigi murmured sympathetically. Enid asked her, "What are

you doing this summer? Do you have a job?"

Gigi dimpled. "Not really. I'll just lie around on the beach, I guess. It's not so easy to find work anyway. Todd can't get anything. He's still interviewing people."

"I'm surprised about Todd," Enid said. "He should know better than to wait till the last minute. He must be slipping from that model boy Hazel keeps telling me about."

"I guess all mothers think that."

As soon as she said it, Gigi blushed and looked down at the table. She was probably thinking of Enid's feelings. It was always going to be like that, Enid reflected. People would always be uneasy.

"Yes, I suppose they do," she said.

Gigi rushed on, trying to smooth the awkwardness. "My stepmother's impossible with Drew. She's always fussing, like he's the center of the world. I mean, he's my brother and I love him, but let's face it. Not everybody's so engrossed as she is. Besides, she spoils him rotten. If she keeps it up, nobody's going to love him. Except her."

"You're right," said Enid. "It doesn't really help." She thought, Was it like that with Billy? Was that what I did?

That was what they said. Frank, Lois, Hazel. Even Dr. Longwort, although his version was a little more elaborate.

But what about Billy? What had he thought? That was the crux of what had happened.

She stood up and opened the cupboard where she had put the cake. It was in a covered glass dish to keep it unspoiled. She lifted it down from the shelf and wondered if she had put on enough decorations.

"He was much cuter when he was born," Gigi was saying. "Don't you think newborns are cute? They look so wise and self-contained, almost as if they came from another planet. What's that, a cake?"

She had an interesting vocabulary for a teenager, Enid thought. But then, her father was an English professor.

"Yes," she told the girl. "It's for later, but I'll save you a piece if you want to come tomorrow. I was just getting it down because I have to take it with me. And I agree with you about newborns."

She did not want to think about Billy when he was born.

"Where are you going?" Gigi asked.

"Oh, not right away, but soon. I'm going to a birthday party. All by myself."

"Is it your birthday?"

"No." Enid held herself in. "It's Billy's." And she began to cry.

CHAPTER 9

They were sitting at the dining table with Drew in his high chair. Kurt had suggested that Debra feed him earlier so they could have an adult meal. He seemed to consider Gigi an adult.

"Then I'd have to sit through two dinners," Debra had protested. "And what would we do with him while we're eating? Besides, it's good for him to learn to be with the family."

Kurt had scowled and replied, "Then it's too bad he can't learn to emulate our table manners."

"He's only a baby! Give him time."

It was not so much the spilling and the mess that he objected to, Kurt explained, although they were indeed objectionable. It was the domination that really got to him. The way Drew took over an entire meal.

"This is what I mean," he said as Drew pushed away his dish and began to raise his voice in loud complaint. "How can anybody carry on a civilized conversation?"

"He'll learn," Debra promised. "But he won't learn if he has to eat by himself. What is it, Drewie? Don't you want your peas? How about one more bite?" She took the spoon from his hand, scooped up three peas, and aimed it toward his mouth, which clamped shut.

"That's the domination I was talking about," said Kurt. "He breaks into everything with his own demands, and immediately you start catering—"

Debra felt a hot flush of irritation and despair. "I was trying to keep him quiet. I thought that's what you wanted."

"Then put him in his room."

"I don't want him up there by himself when we're down here. He could fall down the stairs. I liked our nice little apartment. I knew what was going on in that place."

Kurt mopped his forehead with a paper napkin. They were growing heated, and Gigi looked from one to the other, her eyes glittering with pleasure.

"I'm sorry," Debra said. "I just wish this house were a little more compact, like that place the Mauls live in."

"I never thought you'd complain about a big house," said Kurt. "This happens to be what was available, and I thought it would be nice to have the space for a change. I thought you'd like it, too."

"Oh, I do. It's just that it's so . . . hard to watch him."

And there was a lot to keep tidy, and it would be drafty in winter. She couldn't tell him how much she disliked it.

Gigi, brimming with an excitement which she had been suppressing for quite a while, said, "I was in that house today. The Mauls'. I found out why they had to give up this one and move back there to get more money. I found out what they need it for."

Kurt obliged her with a grudging, "All right, what?"

He likes her better than Drew, Debra thought. It was true that Gigi behaved better, but probably Kurt preferred her because she was a girl and played up to him.

"I found out," Gigi announced dramatically, "that Billy Maul is still alive."

"Is alive?" her father repeated in bewilderment.

"What do you mean?" asked Debra.

"He didn't die when he shot himself. He was in a coma for a long time and then he came out of it. He has a lot of brain damage, though. I mean, he shot himself in the head. He'll probably never be right again, but he's getting therapy."

Debra remembered the feeling she had had about the place. The feeling that something was there. Or that something would happen.

"Where . . . is he?" she asked.

"In a nursing home," said Gigi. "That's why they need the money. Nursing homes are expensive."

"Don't I know," said Kurt, whose father had been in one. "I shouldn't think the rent we pay would even begin to cover it."

"Oh, it doesn't. That's why they want to get him out," Gigi explained. "He's going to start coming home on weekends, starting this week. Today was his birthday," she added.

"Coming home?" asked Debra.

Gigi looked indignant. "Why not? He has a right. And they have a right, too. After all, he's their son. What if it was Drew?"

"Don't say that!" Debra could not bear the girl's expression. She knew Gigi delighted in making her uncomfortable.

"What's wrong?" Gigi asked innocently. "Are you afraid he's going to be dangerous, or something?"

"I just don't know."

It wasn't that, Debra told herself. It was the thought of seeing him, and thinking of Enid Maul, who was also a mother, and how Billy had once been a baby like Drew, and you never could tell what might happen in life.

"Well," said Kurt, setting down his fork, "I think that's good news. I don't mean the fact that he's brain-damaged, but that he's alive at all. As the saying goes, where there's life, there's hope. At least, more than . . . the other way."

"Me, too," Gigi agreed, and glanced again at Debra. "I feel kind of relieved. Except I wonder how it is for him, knowing what he did to himself."

Debra mopped Drew's face and removed him from his highchair. She dampened a corner of the kitchen towel to clean his face still further and helped him wash his hands at the sink.

She marveled at his plump little hands. Did Billy Maul once have hands like that?

Drew was so precious. She could not bear the thought that anything bad might happen to him, ever.

How can I keep him safe? she wondered.

Drew said, "Go see the water."

"Do you want to go to the beach, Kurt?" Debra asked. "It might be nice now in the evening, and you haven't been there all day."

"Not particularly," he replied. "I don't mind going out for some air, though. Shall we take a short walk?"

Gigi declined to go with them. Kurt and Debra set out with Drew, who danced happily, glad to be going anywhere with his parents.

When they reached the sidewalk, instead of turning toward the beach, Kurt stood surveying the length of Angel Road. "I wonder what's up that way."

"But Drew wanted—" Debra stopped herself. "I think it's mostly houses."

Then she remembered the grave.

"Gigi says there's an old grave. It's what Angel Road is named after."

"The grave of an angel?"

"That's what's written on it. Todd showed it to her."

"Is this Todd going to hang around all summer?" asked Kurt. "He's a lot older than she is, isn't he?"

"Yes. Nineteen."

"What does he see in a kid who's got two more years of high school?"

"She's very attractive, Kurt."

"I don't like it. I'd rather see her with a bunch of kids her own age."

"She really doesn't know any," Debra pointed out. "It would be different if she went to school here. Maybe she'll meet some at the beach."

"That seems natural." Kurt was satisfied. They had, after all, been there only a few days.

She knew they were coming to the grave when she saw a cluster of trees. And a weeping willow. It was almost like a little park.

They stood at the rail, trying to read the inscription on the lone gravestone.

"Interesting," said Kurt.

Drew tried to hoist himself over the rail.

"Drewie, be careful!" Debra reached out, but Kurt caught her arm.

"Let him take a few tumbles. You damage a kid's self-esteem when you rescue him all the time."

"But he's only a baby." She watched in trepidation as Drew slipped down over the rail, landing on his knees, then picked himself up and galloped across the grass.

"When does he stop being a baby?" Kurt took her elbow, and they stepped over the railing to follow their son.

"I don't know," she admitted. "But they do grow up, and you let go a little more each time."

"Well, I think he's already not a baby. I think you're too involved with him and you should learn to back off sometimes. Let him experience the rest of the world."

She knew all that, in a way, but Drew was *hers*. She felt somehow that Kurt was trying to take him away, the only thing that was hers. Telling her to back off.

And yet she knew she must. But she wasn't ready. He was only a baby.

"'Here lies an angel,'" Kurt read from the gravestone. "'William Cotsworth Darnley. Eighteen forty-four to eighteen forty-seven.' My God, that was before the Civil War."

"Three years old," Debra said huskily. And she remembered what else Gigi had told her. Todd had asked how old Drew was, and said . . .

Kurt, his arms folded, stood gazing up at the trees. There was a contented smile on his face. He wasn't thinking of the grave, or of Drew, or Debra . . .

"Are you happy here?" she asked.

"You mean right here on this spot?"

"I mean in Luna Beach. You look happy right now."

"Don't you think that's good? To be happy?" He smiled. Dreamily. Kurt was not a dreamy type.

"Yes, I guess so," she said.

"Isn't that what we all want?" He guided her back to the street. "Come on. We've seen history. I guess it's time to take the kid to his water."

"Come on, Drewie." She reached for his hand. "We're going to see the water."

Drew capered happily, trying to run past them. She seized his arm. She was not ready to let him go.

Kurt walked beside her, not touching her, but her elbow still tingled from the feel of his hand. It had been a tender gesture.

She turned cold when she remembered the way he had

smiled up at the trees. It was only a faint smile, but it told her more than she wanted to know.

It had been like that before. On Long Island. When he first met that Stacie woman. Debra hadn't known at the time what was going on, but later she put it all together.

And it was happening again. She had had fair warning that night at the reception, but then he threw her off with his sweetness and the flowers.

They crossed the street and walked on. Her legs moved automatically. Drew tried to pull away from her, not wanting to be confined, but she held tightly.

She saw the name Jorgenson burned into a wooden sign. Their house was apple green with white shutters. The woman was divorced and had been for a long time, but she still had her son. What would she do when Todd wanted to leave home? When he took a job somewhere, or got married?

On the next block was the Mauls' cottage, with their two cars parked outside. As she watched, a blue station wagon came up the driveway. Debra recognized Enid Maul's sister, who had sat with her under the trees, and their two girls. This time the husband was with them.

When they reached their own house, Drew pulled toward the fence. She was pleased that he recognized it.

"We're going to see the water, Drewie," she said. He danced at the end of her arm like a monkey on a string.

She remembered what Hazel Jorgenson had said about the Mauls. About the girl at the bank. Hazel had implied that it was because Enid was too involved with their son, and growing tiresome.

But maybe that wasn't the reason, Debra thought. Some men were just like that. And maybe the tragedy with their son made it all the worse. It made Enid bitter.

Kurt asked, "What's with this silence?"

"You're not exactly talkative yourself," she said. But for a different reason. His preoccupation came from happiness. "I was thinking, that's all."

"About?"

"Everything."

It was all tumbling through her mind, about Kurt and Mr. Maul, and how she did not want to be like Enid. About how Drew would grow up and she couldn't keep him safe forever.

And the little boy found on the beach with his neck broken. And Billy Maul . . . It was all so unbearable.

She picked up Drew and carried him, in spite of Kurt's disapproval, holding him close, feeling his small, soft body against hers.

CHAPTER 10

Lois Claridge embraced her sister. "We just came to cheer you up, darling."

"For what?" Enid scarcely needed to ask. Probably Frank was in on it, too.

"Because it's . . . you know." Lois smiled uneasily. "Did you see him today?"

"Of course I did." Enid would not tell them she had taken a cake to the nursing home. They would think that was silly.

"How is he?"

"About the same. Apathetic." She had tried so hard to get him to talk. Even to make a sound.

The doctor had recommended speech therapy. That would be still more expense. She would have to take a full-time job, and then how could she care for him at home?

Frank lit a fire in the barbecue, while Lois and her daughters brought foil-covered dishes from the car.

"Macaroni salad," Lois ticked off. "Green salad for vitamins. Chocolate cake."

It was a frosted cake in a square pan. Lois had remembered Billy's fondness for chocolate.

"This is sweet of you," Enid said. She watched Robin and Vicky help their mother set up the table. They were tanned and skinny-legged in their shorts. And Lois knew they would never put a gun to their heads.

"Enid, how about a beer?" asked Frank. They were all making merry while they waited for the fire to be ready.

"No, thanks."

"A little wine?"

"Nothing. Really."

Lois suggested asking Hazel to come over.

"No," said Enid quickly.

"Why? Are you mad at her or something?" Lois asked.

"No, I just don't want her."

"I'll bet it kind of hurts to see Todd walking around."

"He has a right to," Enid replied. "It's not his fault. But Hazel's just tiresome, that's all."

Lois understood only too well. "I guess we all came down on you pretty hard."

"I still think," said Enid, "it was an ego trip, all that assumption of superiority."

"That's not the way it was," Lois argued. "I really was trying to help you."

"And I suppose Hazel was, too, with all that bragging about how she raised the wonder scholar all by herself? Forget it."

Lois leaned toward her and asked in a low voice, "Did you talk about any of this with You Know Who?"

"Some."

"What did he say?"

"That's privileged information."

Frank turned from poking his fire. "Who's that? Who are you talking about?"

He sounded nervous, and Enid was pleased. Did he really believe that she, too, might have a lover somewhere?

Lois said, "Oh, just somebody."

But Enid, not wanting to seem tarnished, explained. "Lois thought I should go and see a shrink, so I did. I don't think it helped any."

"You only saw him once," Lois reminded her.

Frank said, "I don't believe in shrinks."

Lois gave a tight laugh. "That's pretty dumb. They *are* real. It's not like not believing in unicorns, for instance."

Vicky piped up, "Even unicorns are real. It's a kind of fish that has a horn just like that."

"A mammal," said her father. "A sea mammal." He took over the fire and tried to defuse everybody. "Think it's ready for the steak yet?"

"Just about." Frank unwrapped the meat.

"Oh, we brought fried onion rings," said Lois. "Enid, do you have a can opener and a dish?"

"Out of a can?" asked Frank.

"Why?" said Lois. "Does Enid make her own? With coating? These have coating. Well, Enid always was a gourmet cook. I just don't have the time."

Frank looked over at Enid and winked. He knew she made a special effort with her cooking. She felt a glow of pleasure. He so rarely showed his appreciation.

The steak began to sizzle. Arnold Claridge leaned back his head and inhaled the aroma. Lois removed the foil from her dishes and exclaimed at the presence of an early yellow jacket.

"I thought they didn't come until August," she said.

"A bee!" screeched Robin.

"Don't get excited, honey." Arnold put an arm around his daughter.

Enid watched them with envy. If only Frank had been able

to show that kind of tenderness with Billy.

Instead, Frank had insisted that Billy should be a man, even when he was still small. It was really because Frank could not be tender, as Arnold could. It was a matter of upbringing, she supposed.

And yet he had winked at her. Maybe sometimes he tried.

Frank and Arnold worked over the steak, each with his own notion of how it should be done. Finally it was ready, sliced, and served.

Enid found she wasn't hungry. She thought of Billy at the nursing home and how he had stared without expression when she showed him the cake. She had tried to feed him a piece, but he hadn't wanted it. Because he was so inactive, she told herself. It killed a person's appetite. But she had the feeling that she was only annoying him.

The chatter swirled around her. She paid no attention, except to look up at the sound of a car.

It was Todd's old black sedan, and it stopped at the Gillises'. Why did he have to drive over when he lived on the next block? He was taking that girl somewhere.

It should have been Billy going out with a girl.

She had encouraged Billy to date. She had never tried to deprive him of having a life of his own, as Dr. Longwort seemed to think.

But how did Billy see it? Maybe she came on a little too intensely in her love for him. Maybe he misunderstood and thought she was smothering him. It was hard to tell how one's very sincere motives might appear to someone else.

A light laugh floated across the yard as Gigi came out of the house with Todd. Gigi waved to the gathering and Enid waved back.

"Who's that?" asked Lois. "Is that the stepdaughter?"

Enid felt unaccountably annoyed. "It all depends on who

you're talking about. She's Dr. Gillis's *real* daughter." And at that she realized how much she hated Debra, with her blobby little child.

Lois, unaware, remarked, "Todd didn't waste any time, did he?"

"He wouldn't," said Frank.

Enid watched them leave. She felt sad. Never again would Billy take out a pretty girl on a summer evening.

But it was more than that. She felt sad for Todd and Gigi, and she did not know why.

CHAPTER 11

"Todd, this is cool!" Gigi managed to overlook the car's somewhat tattered interior. "Is it really yours? It's almost a limousine. I love big cars, don't you? And I love driving at night. I wish it would get dark."

"Big cars eat a lot of gas." After three starts, he coaxed the engine into running. "What's all that gang over at the Mauls' house?"

"It's Billy's birthday, didn't you know? He's supposed to be your friend."

"Yeah, but . . . What are they doing, having a party? How can you have a party for a guy who isn't there?" He turned his car down Barton Avenue toward the main part of town.

"In absentia," Gigi said. "We celebrate George Washington's birthday every year. And Jesus Christ's. And Lincoln."

"But not a party."

"Christmas is a party, lots of times. Anyhow, I wonder why they didn't wait. He'll be there this weekend."

"Who will?"

"Billy. Didn't they tell you? He's going to start coming home on weekends."

Todd stopped with a jolt at a traffic light that was turning red. His car jutted into the intersection, forcing him to back.

"Yeah?" he said. "Old Billy's coming home? I thought he was going to be in that place forever."

"Oh, no, it's too expensive. They're going to try to get him out, if they can."

"Where'd you hear that?"

"From Mrs. Maul. Todd, do you have any—"

"We're going to the beach," he said.

"For swimming?"

"Don't be dumb. I have to see somebody first. Then we'll park at the Grand Union and go over to the water."

"Why the Grand Union?"

"Because we can't park on the street. Anytime between Memorial Day and Labor Day, you can't park on the street." He chuckled. "It used to get Bill in a lot of trouble."

"Billy Maul? How come?"

Todd laughed out loud. "Finding a parking space. Sometimes people kill over parking spaces."

Gigi was shocked. "He didn't do that, did he?"

"No, he did better. He wanted to park at his dad's office, but the old man wouldn't let him. So he'd park where he could, and he got tickets. He must have run up a few hundred dollars."

Gigi, too, began to laugh. "What did his dad say about that?"

"He blew his top. But after that, the old lady paid them."

"So his dad didn't know? Then what was the point?"

Todd shrugged. "You never know about Bill. He was weird."

They stopped on a side street and Todd went into a magazine and candy store. A moment later he returned, carrying a paper bag.

From there they drove to the supermarket, parked the car, and went inside to buy cold sodas.

The store was crowded and they waited in the express line for several minutes. Todd read aloud from the tabloids at the checkout counter.

"Look, here's a guy who kept his wife in a freezer."

"That's disgusting," said Gigi.

"What's the difference? She was dead. You couldn't keep anybody alive in a freezer. Hey, get this one. 'Eight-year-old has baby with two heads.'"

"Todd, please, it's making me sick."

"I don't know where they dream up these things. Probably have a staff of idea people. They must give themselves a lot of laughs. And the guys who fake the photos. I'll bet they could put Bill Maul in some of these." He pushed his two soda cans toward the checker.

"I thought Billy was your friend," Gigi said.

"He was. I mean, he is. But you should have seen him. He can't have a brain left in his head."

Gigi never liked it when people joked about such things. She thought of going home by herself, but it was too far and she didn't know how. Besides, she needed Todd.

They walked two blocks to the beach, through a mixed neighborhood of shops and small houses. She felt edgy and irritable, but still curious.

"Do you mean you *saw* Billy?" she asked. "When he shot himself?"

"Sure. Afterward."

"I didn't know that."

"There was old Enid screaming and screaming. You couldn't help knowing."

"You could hear her all the way from your house?"

"Not my house. Theirs," he said. "I came over to ask Billy

something and I heard her screaming."

"What did you do?"

"I could see him. Through the basement window. At first I thought he blew his head right off."

"How did you know what happened?"

"Hell, he was lying there with blood all over and a gun in his hand."

She could almost see Todd peering through the window, which was close to the ground, and Mrs. Maul screaming.

"I didn't know you were there," she said again.

"I wasn't, exactly. I was outside."

"But the basement's kind of dark. How could you see?"

"He had the light on."

"If I were going to shoot myself," Gigi decided, "I think I'd have it off. I'd rather do it in the dark."

"That's up to you."

They clambered down a retaining wall to the beach. It had soft sand, but was narrow and unkempt, full of debris and broken shells. Some distance away, a sea wall jutted into the water to prevent further erosion. Several people were fishing from it.

"Did you go and help her?" Gigi asked.

"Who?" Todd found a log that had washed ashore, and they sat down.

"Mrs. Maul."

"I went home and called the police," he said. "But I guess she already called them. I didn't go in because I thought he was dead. There was nothing I could do."

"I like Mrs. Maul."

"Yeah, she's okay."

"I wonder why he did it."

"He probably doesn't remember. I heard he's pretty much a vegetable."

Todd seemed in no hurry for anything. She stood it as long as she could, perhaps thirty seconds, and then said, "I thought we came here for a reason."

"What's the matter, you getting jumpy?"

"I've been jumpy all afternoon. Don't you have anything? What's in there?" She reached for the paper bag.

He held it away from her.

"Come on, Todd."

"I can't go on giving it to you for free," he said. "You know that. You ought to know."

"I do. I'll get some money."

"How?"

"I'll ask my dad. Or mom. I'll get it."

"How long do you expect me to wait? Gigi, I'm in trouble. I owe somebody five thousand dollars. I need it *now*. If you pay me, then I can give him something to shut him up, anyway."

"I'll get it tomorrow," she said. "Okay?"

He didn't believe her. "What are you going to do, tell your dad what you want it for?"

"I'll think of something."

Todd grinned. "I've got a better idea."

"Oh, no. I'll get it from my dad."

"How do you know what I was going to say?"

"Because I just know."

She began to shiver. Somewhere in her mind she had known this might happen, but she had thought she could manage. She thought she had time.

In a small voice she asked, "Can I please have some now, if I promise?"

"Promises are no good," he said. "I can't pay with promises."

"I know, Todd, but please? I'm going crazy."

"How did you get on this stuff, anyway?"

"Please?"

"I asked you a question."

"I don't know," she said miserably. "Everybody was doing it. They wouldn't leave me alone."

"How do you pay for it at home?"

"Different ways. I can usually find money around the house. But I didn't need so much then. It's gotten worse."

"You always need more, not less," he said.

"I *know*. Todd, I promise. Tomorrow, okay?"

"Okay."

But he still made her wait. And suffer. He took an endless time digging through the pockets of a jacket he had brought, first finding a mirror, then a razor blade, and then a straw that was still in its Burger King wrapper.

They sat close together facing the ocean, so no one could see them from the street. Carefully he arranged the powder into neat, thin lines on the mirror's surface, and then inhaled it with a straw. She watched avidly, thinking he was going to take it all, but finally he passed the mirror and the straw to her.

"Thank you, Todd. I would have died," she said when she had finished.

"No, you wouldn't."

"I *would*. And I'll get you the money tomorrow."

She didn't know how. She would deal with that later. In the meantime, she waited for the glorious rush that made it all bearable.

Todd reached around in back of her.

She expected to feel his arm drawing her close. Instead, something icy touched her shoulder. She jumped up, crying out.

He laughed. It was only his soda can.

"I should have known," she said, smiling ruefully. "I guess I got spooked after all that talk about . . . you know."

"You thought it was Billy coming to get you?"

"He's not dead."

"He'll be a zombie," said Todd. "There isn't anything left. He'll probably stalk the neighborhood and eat little children."

"Don't say that."

"It's true. He already did it, even when he was alive."

"He's still alive," said Gigi. "What are you talking about?"

"Nothing. I shouldn't have said that. Billy's my pal."

"What do you mean, Todd?"

"I told you, forget it. Anyway, I don't know. I just saw him once. Never mind. Let's go eat something."

They drove to Roy Rogers for hamburgers and shakes, and ate sitting in the car.

"What were you saying about Billy Maul?" she asked. "What did you see him do?"

"Nothing," Todd said quickly.

"I wish you wouldn't start these things." She kicked at the floorboard. "Did Billy use?"

"Not that I know of. And I would have known."

"If he did, I could understand what happened. Back there when you wouldn't give it to me, I really got to thinking about killing myself. Then I wouldn't have to go through that again."

"Is it that bad?"

"No. I just thought about it."

"You'd better remember, Gigi. If there's no money tomorrow, we'll have to work out something else."

"I told you, I'll have it for you."

Somehow. But she would not turn any tricks for him, if that was what he meant. And it must have been. A lot of girls were driven to that, but not her. Not yet. Still, she knew there would come a time when it might not even matter.

Todd started the car and they drove around aimlessly, weaving back and forth among the shore streets.

"All these houses look empty," she said.

"Not all," he replied, "but a lot of them are. Most of the ones along here are vacation homes. The people come down later, about July."

"If I had a house near the beach, I'd stay in it all year."

"They should. They might not get ripped off so much. Empty houses get ripped off. Do you want to go back to the beach?"

"Let's drive till it gets dark, and then go."

"It's almost dark now," he said.

"Not quite." There was still a glow in the sky. A beautiful twilight glow. And a warm wind on her face. She loved it. She didn't even mind going back to the beach with him. She didn't care what he meant to do there.

"You know, Todd? I forgot to notice when the sun went down. We could have watched it from the beach."

"The beach is east," he reminded her.

"We can watch it on Long Island. But it's way over on the side. Long Island goes sideways. I mean, it slants."

He did not seem to care very much. She couldn't blame him. She asked, "Doesn't your car have a radio?"

"It broke."

She knew it hadn't broken. He had sold it. She knew about those things.

He asked, "Do you have any sisters?"

"No. Just twin brothers. And Drew. My mom and stepdad had twins."

"Yeah?"

"Five years old. They're brats. I always wanted an older brother."

"Too bad," he said.

They reached the shore again, at nearly the same spot where

they had been earlier. Todd pulled into a parking area behind a restaurant, ignoring the sign that said, "Mario's Seafood. Parking for Patrons Only."

They crossed the street and scrambled down the embankment once more. This time the beach was dark and secret. The lights from the restaurant did not reach it.

They left their shoes by the wall and she giggled, hoping they would be able to find them later. As they walked toward the water, Todd put his arm around her. She slipped hers around his waist. She liked the feel of his body, so big and solid. He smelled nice, too. It was not cologne, but a nice, clean smell. Maybe soap.

She looked for the log they had sat on before. Todd didn't want to sit. He began to massage her back.

Then he turned her so that they were face to face. He had a hard-on already. She could feel it.

Gently she eased herself out of his embrace. Still holding his hand, she moved to the very edge of the water. He did not protest or try to pull her back. They stood letting the foam wash over their toes.

She sighed and rested her head against his shoulder. Watching the bubbles, she felt as though she could float away. Keep floating into the far reaches of space.

His hand began to work at her upper arm, then slipped down toward her breast.

"Gigi," he murmured into her ear. "Where'd you get a silly name like that?"

"Short for Giselle. It's my initials, too. Giselle Gillis."

He kissed her forehead. "You're going to be mine, Gigi. You know that? All mine."

"All your what?" She tried to laugh, but he seemed so intense that it frightened her.

He didn't answer. He said, "Come on. Get wet," and tried to pull her into the water.

She giggled. "I don't want to get wet. It's cold."

"It's not cold. Not after you're in it."

"It's *cold*, Todd. It makes my legs ache."

"It'll wake you up. Come on."

She gasped. The water was icy. It made her ache all over. And he was right. It woke her up.

Her jeans clung soggily to her legs. She gave another gasping laugh, thinking that when she came out of the water soaking wet, there would be no way to get dry and she would freeze.

He pulled her forward, his arm still clamped around her.

"I told you you're mine. You do what I say."

"Are you trying to drown me?" she screeched.

It was just a silly game. But he was high and had lost his judgment.

"You can't do this." Laughing, she tried to pull herself free.

His hand tightened on her wrist. They were in water up to their thighs, and splashed by every breaking wave.

Then a higher wave came. It caught her and lifted her. Todd's hold on her broke.

The wave set her down heavily and drained past her, trying to pull her with it. She was wet nearly up to her chin.

"Hey!" she said, and struggled toward the shore. For a moment she couldn't see Todd.

Another wave crashed, knocking her down. She fought against the boiling, swirling cold. A violent force pulled her outward into deep water.

She kicked against the pull. Her kick was feeble. Water filled her mouth and nose.

Then something caught her arm.

A human hand. It clamped around her waist and lifted her from the water.

She coughed and choked, trying to catch her breath. There was air around her now instead of water. Her feet were on dry sand.

She couldn't breathe. She fought, but could not take in air.

Todd pounded her back. She choked again. He pounded until, with a labored gasp, she caught a very small breath.

It wasn't enough. She grew frantic and tried to breathe again. She sank to her knees.

Finally her lungs filled. She took one breath after another in heavy, noisy, wheezing gasps. She knelt doubled over. Todd's hand was on her shoulder.

"You have to watch that undertow," he said.

She shook her head. It had not been her idea to go into the water.

He pulled her upright. "You okay?"

She tried to look at him and choked again.

His mouth found hers, in spite of the choking.

She pushed him away. She didn't want to be kissed when she was still struggling to breathe.

He caught her and pulled her toward him. He kissed her forehead, her nose, her mouth. She felt the hard-on again, and recoiled. He took her hand and guided it downward.

Please. No. She had almost drowned. She wasn't ready.

"Gigi," he said. "You're mine. Remember?"

Taking him by surprise, she twisted away. As he came at her again, she aimed her knee at his groin.

He folded over and stumbled away from her.

She was stricken. What had she done?

"I'm . . . sorry, Todd."

She had no voice.

Groaning, he moved toward her again.

She held out her arms, trying to fend him off. He caught her and threw her onto the sand.

She struggled. His hands clamped around her throat.

She pounded at him. Scratched at the face that grimaced in rage. She kicked and squirmed, trying to breathe, but his weight was on her.

Then she felt her arms drop helplessly. His face disappeared as the night roared around her.

CHAPTER 12

Enid pushed her cart down the supermarket aisle, looking for the things Billy liked. He would be home that evening. Friday night.

It wouldn't be like before. He would not be the real Billy, the one she had lost. He was almost a travesty of Billy. But she would keep working with him until he was as close to normal as he could get.

"Oh, Enid!"

It was Hazel Jorgenson. She wore a magenta dirndl this time, and pushed a grocery cart stacked with frozen dinners.

"I'm looking for lasagna noodles," Enid said. "Billy always liked lasagna."

An odd look crossed Hazel's face. Probably she thought Enid was demented.

"He's coming home, you know," Enid told her. "He'll be coming home every weekend, starting tonight."

Hazel stared for a moment, then broke into a smile.

"How wonderful! Oh, darling, I'm so happy for you."

Enid found the noodles.

"It's not wonderful. It's just the best we can do."

"Wait till Todd hears about this," said Hazel. "He'll be so glad to see Billy again."

Enid did not reply. If Todd had really wanted to see Billy, he could have visited him in the nursing home.

Lest Hazel think there had been a complete recovery, she explained, "Billy's not the same. He can't get around very well. He's in a wheelchair a lot of the time. And he can't talk yet."

"Can't talk?"

"He's brain-damaged. You know that. But we're thinking of getting speech therapy."

"I hope it all works out, Enid. I know it will."

"I don't know that it will, but I hope so," Enid replied. She knew she ought to be polite. "How's Todd doing? Did he find a job yet?"

"Not yet. He goes out and sees people, but nothing's come through. I don't really think it's so awful if he takes the summer off. I keep telling him his main job right now is getting educated, preparing for the future."

Hazel stopped short and looked embarrassed. She probably remembered that Billy had no future.

"It's all right, Hazel," Enid said. "I know what's what. You don't have to pussyfoot."

Hazel smiled uneasily. "When did you say Billy's coming?"

"Tonight."

"I'm so glad. Are you and Frank going there to get him?"

"Well, he's not going to drive himself, that's for sure," Enid said. "His coordination isn't good yet."

"I'll bet Frank's excited." Hazel picked up a box of rigati and studied the recipes on the back.

"Very." Enid tried to imagine Frank being excited about anything.

103

Hazel set down the box and picked up another.

"The things that go on in this town. I'm telling you." There was a purr in her voice that put Enid on guard. "Do you want to hear a piece of gossip?"

Enid sighed. "I guess I'm going to."

Hazel moved closer.

"You know that teller at the bank? The McCoy girl with the long black hair who used to be a cheerleader? I hear she's in the family way."

Enid went stiff. She clutched at her cart, betraying nothing.

"What's so unusual?" she managed to ask.

There was scarcely any use in bluffing. Of course Hazel knew about Frank and the girl. Otherwise, why would she have bothered to mention it?

Hazel did her best to explain. "I just thought it was sort of interesting. You know. It's somebody we see every day . . ."

"It happens all the time," said Enid.

"Doesn't it? Really. Anyhow, I feel sorry for her. I wonder what she's going to do."

Enid consulted her shopping list. The sauce was farther down the aisle. She tried to squeeze her cart past Hazel's. But Hazel was transfixed, watching for a reaction, and did not move.

"I have to get going, dear," Enid told her. "It always takes me a while to make lasagna."

"Oh, me, too." Hazel moved her cart, but not enough.

"How are the new tenants working out?" she asked. "Is Frank pleased?"

"Ecstatic." Enid knew very well that Hazel was simply refusing to drop the subject of Frank.

"Tell him I said hello, will you?"

"I certainly will. Have yourself a nice day, Hazel."

By concentrating on her list and nothing else, Enid was able to finish her shopping and get everything into the car.

It could stay there for a while, she decided. All the cold things were packed together. They would last, if she parked in the shade. It was clouding over anyway. And there was no ice cream or anything perishable.

She drove to Frank's office and parked in back of it under a large tree. For the first time, as she looked up at the tree, she realized that some of its branches nearly touched the bank next door.

The bank where Marianne McCoy worked. It seemed almost a symbolic joining of the two, Frank's parking lot and Marianne's bank.

She entered the office building through a rear door. Grace April, one of the secretaries, looked up from her filing.

"Enid! I didn't know you were coming in today."

Enid spoke hurriedly. "I'm not, really. I just want to see Frank. Is he here?"

Without waiting for an answer, she went to Frank's office. He was there, talking on the telephone. She closed the door and sat down to wait. He glanced at her with a bemused frown and went on talking.

Finally he was finished.

"Surprised to see you here," he said. "I thought you'd be home getting ready for Bill."

"I was. I've just been shopping and I met Hazel."

"Anything wrong?"

"Not about Billy, no. I want you to come and have coffee with me, Frank. I don't want to talk in here."

"Enid, I can't just pick up and leave right now. I have . . ." He waved a hand at the clutter on his desk.

"Just for a little while. I want to get something straight or I'm going to be a wreck all day."

What she would be if it all turned out to be true, she had not

105

yet decided. She only wanted to know the facts.

He tried again. "Can't it wait till I get home?"

"I just told you. I have to know now."

"Enid . . ."

"*Now*, Frank."

He knew, she thought. He guessed what she wanted to talk about. Grumbling, he went to his private bathroom and straightened his hair and tie. After giving instructions to the staff that he would be back in a little while, he left with Enid.

They crossed the street to a small luncheonette. The waitresses knew both of them, which made her think that he probably never went there with Marianne. There were booths against the wall, and they could talk quietly.

Frank ordered their coffee at the counter and carried it over to the booth where Enid waited.

"Do you want anything to eat with that?" he asked.

"No, I don't feel like eating."

He sat down opposite her and poured sugar into his coffee. "Okay, Enid, what is it?"

She concentrated on stirring her own coffee, although there was nothing to stir. She didn't use sugar, but it kept her from having to look at him.

"I want to know about that girl," she said.

"What girl?"

"Okay, Frank, if we're going to play games. That girl at the bank. The one with the long black hair, as Hazel says."

"What's Hazel got to do with it?" he asked.

"Hazel's the one who told me there's going to be a blessed event. Is that right?"

He said nothing.

"Is that right, Frank?"

He shifted his position, knocking the table with his knees. Her coffee slopped back and forth in its cup but did not spill.

"What the hell," he asked again, "has Hazel got to do with it?"

"Well, you know Hazel. She couldn't wait."

"I still don't understand."

"Look, Frank, I don't know how she knew, but if she did, it seems likely a lot of other people do, too. McCoy probably went to a doctor and somebody saw her there."

He winced at the mention of anything so specific as a name.

"That's not my problem," Enid went on. "My problem is that everybody knows about you and McCoy—"

"Everybody?" he asked sarcastically.

"Everybody. This isn't some big, anonymous city where people don't know people. Everybody knows you've been fooling around with her, and now if she's pregnant it must be your kid, unless she fools around with a lot of people."

"Don't talk like that," he warned her.

"All right, I won't, as if talking about it's the bad part. I'm sure she's very pure and chaste and faithful to you."

"Enid, I don't know why you're doing this."

"Don't I have a right to know? You're supposed to be my husband. And you already have a child. You have Billy."

She snatched up her napkin and pressed it to her face.

"Don't you think I always wanted another baby?" She wept. "I feel like such a failure. I wanted another chance to be a mother. But I can't, and now *she's* having your child."

"You're not too old." His face looked pale in the dim light of the booth.

"Maybe not, but it doesn't **happen. It never** happened after Billy. He was my only one and I ruined **his life.**"

"You didn't ruin his life, Enid. He ruined his life."

"That's not what you said before." She tried to dry her eyes, but the tears kept flowing.

Absently Frank poured more sugar into his coffee. "I don't

know what I said before. Anyhow, you meant well."

"That's damning."

"You did your best, the way you saw it."

"But it wasn't enough. It was all wrong."

"Maybe it had nothing to do with you. With us." It was the first time he had ever said that. "Maybe Billy got mixed up with something we don't know about. With drugs, or something."

"But why would he? If he did that, then we still failed."

"Kids have an awful lot of peer pressure . . ."

She interrupted. "I never saw anything like that. I used to read all the articles. He didn't show any of the signs, and I never found stuff in his room."

"That doesn't prove anything," Frank pointed out.

"No, I guess not."

"I have to get back to work," he said. "I'm sorry this had to happen. Especially today. I guess I would have told you myself, anyhow."

"What are you going to do about it?"

"I don't know. It depends on what she wants. One thing I don't think she wants is me, but she'll need money."

"We can't afford any money," said Enid. "It's her fault, too, you know."

"Yes, but it's also my fault. I'll talk to her and we'll try to figure something out."

"You're coming home tonight, aren't you? Billy's going to be there."

"I'll try to make it as soon as I can."

"That doesn't sound like much, Frank. I know you don't really want to see him the way he is. You hardly ever visit the home. But I think you should be able to accept him whatever he's like. He needs it."

"He didn't have to shoot himself," Frank muttered. "It was his choice."

"I know, but that doesn't change what we have to do now. Please, Frank? He's our son. He needs us."

It echoed back to the past, when she had pleaded with Frank to be more emotionally giving. He simply didn't have it in him.

And yet he had managed to get involved with Marianne McCoy. She wondered what they were like together.

"I have to go, too," she said. "I have groceries in the car."

"I'll see you tonight, Enid."

"You'd better come home. In fact, I'd like it if you came early so you could help me go and get him."

"What time are you going?"

"About four, maybe."

"I don't think I can get away that early." He sounded relieved.

"That's right. Leave it all to me. It's nothing new, is it?"

"I pay the bills," he reminded her.

"And that's it? A father's supposed to be more than just a money machine, but okay."

If he was going to be difficult, maybe she didn't want him around. She wanted Billy's homecoming to be as smooth and pleasant as possible.

She didn't go back with him to the office but walked through an alley to the parking lot. She couldn't face the cheerful greetings and the knowing looks. They must all have known about Marianne.

Wearily she got into her car. She felt oddly drained, as though she had been crying for a long, long time.

Her sorrow was gone. Even the pain was gone. There was nothing left except a dull, heavy ache.

CHAPTER 13

Debra was still unpacking and washing the dishes, which seemed to have multiplied since they left their apartment. The hardest were the pots and pans. They were bulky, odd-shaped, and uninteresting.

"I wish this place had a dishwasher," she said as Gigi wandered into the kitchen in her shortie nightgown.

Gigi opened the refrigerator and took out the orange juice, ignoring her. She had been up for an hour, and had done nothing but mope and drink juice.

"I think you should put on some clothes," Debra told her. "What if somebody comes?"

"I don't care." Gigi's voice sounded hoarse.

"Well, I care. Are you getting a cold?"

"No."

"Did you go swimming last night with Todd? Your hair was wet when you came in."

"I got ducked," Gigi answered, and went back to her room.

She and Todd must have had a fight, Debra thought.

Perhaps it was just as well. At Gigi's age, a boyfriend four years older was too old. He was in college. He had probably been around more than Gigi could handle. Maybe even took drugs.

She remembered how strange Gigi had been on the day of the reception. She had tried to tell Kurt, or at least had hinted, but he didn't take her seriously. He could see Drew's faults clearly, it seemed, but was blind when it came to his darling daughter.

Debra wondered, with some guilt, if perhaps he was reacting to her own obvious favoritism.

She heard a whistle outside. It was Todd, crossing the driveway. He knocked at the kitchen door.

"Gigi up yet?"

"She's not feeling very well," Debra said.

"Yes, I know. She got knocked down by a wave. I should have warned her about that undertow."

"So that's what happened."

"Yeah." He grinned. "We were just fooling around, not really swimming. I pulled her out, but she got a lot of water up her nose. That can hurt for a while. I've done it myself."

"I'll tell her you're here."

Debra called through Gigi's closed door. There was no answer. After a moment the door opened and Gigi came out dressed in shorts and a T-shirt.

She eyed her visitor warily. "What do you want, Todd?"

He walked over to her with the easy smile of a man who knows his own charm. Gigi remained unmoved.

Good, it's over, Debra thought, and returned to her pots and pans.

She heard Todd say, "I told you I'd be over. I wanted to see how you're feeling."

"Don't give me that," Gigi answered. They went into her room and closed the door.

Debra clattered the pans loudly to remind them that she was there.

Also to drown them out. There was something about them that made her uneasy. She felt old and on the shelf.

It was because of Kurt. Because he had found someone more desirable. It wasn't fair.

A car went by on the driveway. Enid Maul, probably coming back from shopping. Getting ready for Billy's homecoming.

Debra wondered what Billy was like. What had he been like before he shot himself, and how bad was it now? She hoped she would not have to meet him.

Gigi flung open her door. Todd called, "Hey, wait!" but Gigi ran through the kitchen and across the yard to Enid's house.

Todd made no attempt to follow.

"How are you doing?" he asked Debra.

"Still unpacking." She returned his friendly smile, trying to show that he was welcome in spite of Gigi's behavior.

He squatted on the floor beside Drew. "How's it going, kid?"

Drew glanced at him and went on running his trucks in and out among the crumpled newspapers that had wrapped the pots and dishes.

"Pretty nice stuff you have there. Let me see that."

Reluctantly Drew handed him the cement mixer.

"That's a nice one," Todd said. "It even has a diesel pipe. And the tank really moves."

"Does it bring back your childhood?" Debra asked.

He laughed. "My second childhood, maybe. I don't remember too well."

Drew reached for the truck. "I want it."

"Sure thing." Todd gave it back to him. "You like these things, huh? Cars and trucks and stuff like that?"

Debra said, "He loves them. And boats, too. He loves water toys."

Todd grinned. "Now I know how to make friends with him."

That alarmed her. "Please don't think of giving him anything. He has enough stuff already. You should see the floor of his room sometimes."

"Whatever you say."

She liked his easy manner. His handsome smile. She could understand why Gigi was attracted. And if they had had a falling out, it was probably Gigi's fault. She could be difficult at times.

"How does he like the beach?" asked Todd.

"Very much, but I can't keep him there long. He burns too easily."

"No problem today. It's clouding over. Probably going to rain."

"Oh, is it?" She looked out at the sky. It was bright with high cloudiness. "When's it supposed to start, do you know?"

"This afternoon sometime."

"Oh, darn it." She looked down at her little boy, who stared back with round, dark eyes. "We were going to go later this afternoon. I'm expecting my husband home by lunchtime, and then Drew has to have his nap. But I guess it'll be raining by then."

"Do you want me to take him?" Todd asked eagerly. "Would you trust me with him? We could go now for a little while, if you want."

"That's kind of you." Poor only child, she thought. He probably saw Drew as the sibling he never had. "But I think we'll just wait. He'll be getting cranky soon because it's almost lunchtime. Maybe we can get in an hour after lunch and he could take his nap later."

"Whatever. But anytime you want me to look after him or take him to the beach, I'd be glad to. No charge. I like kids."

"That's awfully nice." Debra looked out again. "I wonder what's keeping Gigi."

"Where'd she go?" asked Todd.

"I thought she went to the Mauls' house. She's gotten to be quite a friend of Mrs. Maul."

"Huh!"

Debra felt compelled to defend Gigi's choice, although she did not know why.

"It's hard for her, probably, with me being not too much older than she is. I don't think she quite sees me as a stepmother, and when she's away from her own mother . . . Well, maybe Enid fills that need for her."

"Oh. Like a mother figure."

"I guess so." But Debra felt hurt and inadequate that Gigi had not even considered turning to her.

"I'd better start pushing along," said Todd. "I'm supposed to see somebody this afternoon about a job."

"You still haven't found one? It must be discouraging," she said.

"It's okay. I'm not about to starve. But it gets to be a pain, making all those phone calls and going to see people. Trouble is, I don't have much to offer. I can drive a car and that's about it."

"Your mother said you used to deliver pizza."

"Yes, but there's nothing open now. It's partly my fault. I was so busy with school I just didn't get myself in gear. I'll be seeing you, Deb—Mrs. Gillis."

"Debra," she said, and they smiled at each other with a new understanding. They were friends.

She cooked hot dogs for lunch, because Drew liked them. Kurt did not arrive when she expected him. She waited and watched the sky. If he didn't hurry, they would have to miss the beach altogether. It would be raining and Drew would be frazzled.

Finally, at twelve-thirty, Kurt's car drove up. He was half an hour late.

"What happened?" Debra asked. "I thought you'd be here at twelve, and we could eat quickly and go to the beach before it rains."

"Couple of students wanted to see me. Scheduling problems." He sat down and eyed without pleasure the hot dogs she set on his plate. "What's that?"

"Instant lunch, so we can get to the beach. I'd have made tuna sandwiches, but Drew won't eat them."

"Where's Gigi?" he asked.

"Last I saw, she was going over to Mrs. Maul's. I didn't call her because she already knew we were eating at twelve. She's in some kind of mood."

With a look of disgust, he spread jalapeño mustard on his hot dogs.

"I'm glad she's not with that Todd kid," he said. "He may not be quite the shining knight she thinks he is."

"What do you mean?"

"I went into Records and Registration and punched a few computer keys . . ."

"Breaking into confidential files?" she asked.

"That's exactly right. I found he's been kicked out for academic failure. All this spring he was on probation, and he couldn't or wouldn't pull himself up. So he's dismissed as of last month."

She felt dizzy. She wondered if Todd knew. But of course they would have told him by now.

"I don't think you're supposed to be looking through those records, are you?" she asked.

"I'm faculty. I have a right to know what's going on."

"But he's not one of your students."

"He's hanging around my daughter."

"You're abusing your privileges, Kurt. That's what I think."

"I'm delighted to have your opinion, dear. Now we'll leave it at that."

It made her uneasy. He had grumbled about Gigi's relationship with Todd, but she hadn't thought he would resort to unethical behavior. She wondered what he meant to do about it. Gigi would scarcely be impressed by his findings.

"Well, you'll be glad to know they weren't on good terms this morning," she said. "I don't know what the fight was about, but that was when she suddenly flew off to Mrs. Maul's."

She looked out at the sky again, hoping to change the subject.

"It's really cloudy now. I thought maybe we could put off Drew's nap for a while and get in a little time at the beach before it rains."

"You go ahead," he told her. "I have to get back to school."

"What for? I thought you didn't have anything this afternoon."

"Meetings and stuff," he answered vaguely. "And students with problems. That's my job, you know. I'm not paid to hang out on the beach."

"Yes, but . . . Oh, well." She felt stung. He seemed to be brushing off her plans, and therefore her, as unnecessary trivia.

And Drew. That was the worst part. She had thought he might want to spend some time with Drew. It would have been fun, the three of them together at the beach.

Kurt finished his lunch and the cup of coffee she made for him, then hurried off to the college as though it had had to suspend operations without him.

She left the dishes in the sink and went over to the Mauls' house, carrying Drew in her arms. It seemed ridiculous to call when they were so close by.

"I'm sorry to bother you," she apologized to Enid, "but is Gigi here? I saw her come this way, and I just wanted to tell her that Drew and I are going to the beach for a while and I'm locking the house. I don't know if she has a key with her."

"She's not here. She was only here for a minute. I don't know where she went." Enid kept her eyes on Debra. She seemed to be making a supreme effort to ignore Drew.

But Drew did not like being ignored. He broke into a smile and said "Hi."

The best Enid could manage was "Hmh." She still did not look at him. Trying to make up for the rebuff, Debra hugged him more tightly and rubbed her cheek against his.

"Well," she said, "if you happen to see her, maybe you could just tell her I'll be back in about an hour. But I don't want to leave the house open."

"You're absolutely right," Enid agreed. "There are too many burglaries. I hope you find her."

Since she was already partway there, Debra went on to the next block, to the Jorgenson house.

There was no answer to her ring. She tried the front door and found it locked.

Neither car was in the driveway or in the detached garage, which stood open. She could not imagine that Gigi would have gone off with Todd, considering her mood that morning.

"Okay, Drewie, that's it," she said, and hurried back home to change.

Before they could start out, a fierce wind began to blow. A loud clap of thunder startled Drew and made him cry.

"I think we'd better close the windows," Debra said, and tried to make it a game. She had scarcely finished the living room when the first heavy drops of rain fell and quickly became a downpour.

CHAPTER 14

Pulling her raincoat tightly around her, Enid dashed for the car.

She slid under the wheel, soaked and yet triumphant. She had gotten this far. It was probably stupid. That was what Frank had told her when she called his office. He said to wait until after the worst of it. But that might not be for hours.

He said he couldn't get away early. He was not going to be there to help her. She had not really expected it. Not when he had McCoy, who was young enough to be his daughter.

Then, too, there was that thing about seeing Billy. He couldn't handle it. He had visited the hospital and the nursing home only a few times, and had had to be dragged there each time.

She drove slowly out to the avenue, nearly blinded by sheets of rain in spite of her wipers going at full speed. Then there was all the wind. A real gale.

They said it would be over by midnight. But by then it would be too late to get Billy, and she wasn't going to wait until tomorrow.

The streets were already flooding in spots. When she glimpsed the ocean, she saw high, angry waves. It made her think of that stupid Gillis woman going to the beach.

She felt an unbidden pang of sympathy, and pushed it away. Debra was a younger version of herself. A woman almost alone, and devoted to her child.

But that child was not Billy. She hated that boy. She hated Debra Gillis.

There were few cars at the nursing home. Nobody wanted to visit on a day like this. She parked as close to the door as she could. If only the weather would calm down a little. This wasn't going to be easy.

She was met by an aide, Sara Harris, who said with a laugh, "Mrs. Maul, we didn't expect you out in this kind of storm."

"As long as it's not a hurricane," Enid replied. Tricklets of water ran down her face and neck. Her coat dripped all over the nice tan carpet in their reception room.

"He's not quite ready," Sara told her, "but we'll see what we can do. I'm not sure he really understands that he's going home. He's been kind of difficult."

Enid removed her coat and shook it before venturing into the vinyl-tiled corridor. Water would make the floor slippery and dangerous.

As they walked down the hall, her nose was assaulted by the characteristic smell of disinfectant and something that was probably urine. The place was immaculately clean, but there were too many incontinents. It pervaded the air.

Billy was sitting up in bed, staring out of the window. He was still in his pajamas.

"Hi, hon." Enid bent to kiss his forehead. His face remained stony. Except for the veiled, expressionless eyes and the lack of animation, he was almost her old Billy. All his light brown hair had grown back, covering the wound. His face was a boyish version of her own. Hers, not Frank's. His eyes were hazel, somewhere between the blue of hers and the brown of Frank's.

"Shall we get you dressed?" she asked. "Did you remember that you're coming home for the weekend?"

He stiffened.

"What's wrong, honey? Don't you want to go home?"

While he couldn't talk or even write his thoughts, he often seemed to understand. It was aphasia, they told her. He simply could not use words. They had no meaning for him. No one could tell whether he was able to process words that he heard. Perhaps his brain translated them incorrectly. She tried again.

"Do you remember home, Billy? It's not the big house where we used to live. Dad and I are in the little one now, and we fixed it up real nice. We have your room all ready for you."

He frowned. His body remained rigid. His arms, down at his sides, were like two boards.

"Come on, let's get ready." She started to unbutton his pajama top. He rolled to one side, away from her.

She heard Dr. Longwort. Lois. Frank. Even Hazel. *It was the only way he could break loose from you.*

Did he really hate her so much?

"I promise I won't bug you," she told him desperately. "But you don't want to stay in this place forever, do you? This is your first step out of here."

She looked up at Sara, who stood watching. "Do you think he understands? Why doesn't he want to go home? It can't be that bad."

Sara shook her head. "I just couldn't tell you, Mrs. Maul. It's so hard to know what they're thinking."

"Billy, honey, it's going to be nice," Enid said. "It's raining now, but tomorrow it'll be clear and you can sit outside. If you want, you can sit in back where nobody will see you."

She reached again for his top button. He tried to push away her hand.

"Billy, I'll show you," she pleaded. "Just give it a try. It won't be as bad as you think. And I . . ." She bent toward his ear. "I made lasagna for your supper tonight."

Again she turned to the aide, terrified that they might change their minds in light of this resistance and decide he should not go with her.

"Will you help me?" she asked. "I think he just doesn't understand. But once I get him home, he'll see it's all right."

Sara seemed hesitant.

Enid said, "He probably just doesn't want to see the place again, but it's a different place. I can't make him understand that. It would be good for him to get out of here. I don't see how anybody can get well with nothing but these walls all the time and that smell."

"What smell? Oh, you mean the disinfectant? Okay, Mrs. Maul, I'll try to get some help." Sara went out to the hall and brought back a male nurse. With three pairs of hands, they managed to get Billy dressed.

Enid felt sorry for him. He finally stopped struggling, but kept shaking his head. He tried to talk. Again she told him that everything would be all right as soon as he was home.

They got him into his wheelchair. She looked out and saw that the violent downpour had settled into a steady rain, although the wind was still strong. They wheeled Billy to the entrance and she went to get her car.

When Billy saw it, he stiffened again. The nurse was dubious. "Are you sure you can handle this?" he asked.

Enid laughed uneasily. "I wish I could take you, too. But I think I have to learn to manage, right?"

"Do you want to call your husband?"

"I already did. He can't make it." She would never tell anyone that Frank didn't want to make it.

They lifted Billy into the front seat and placed his folded wheelchair in back. He was quiet now. It seemed a resigned sort of quiet.

"You'll like our new house," Enid told him as she climbed in beside him. "It's the little one, remember? I fixed it up all different and pretty, and I planted a real nice garden. I think you'll like it, sweetie." Then, remembering Dr. Longwort and the others, she added, "But of course I can't tell you what to like."

Billy glared at her. The nurse and the aide stood watching as she drove away.

The trip home was not a long one. The streets were still flooded and the wind blew fiercely. Enid tried to make conversation.

"It's quite a day, isn't it? I wish it could have been nicer for you. We were having such nice weather before. I told you Dad and I moved into the little house, and we rented out the big one. It's an English professor and his wife. He teaches at the college. They have a very pretty girl, but she's a little young for you. Only fifteen. Sometimes she comes to visit me, but I won't let her see you if you don't want."

She stopped talking, dismayed at what she had said. Everything seemed to remind Billy of his disability. The college he had once attended. The pretty girl he couldn't have. The fact that he might not want to be seen.

He stared sullenly at the dashboard, giving no indication that he had heard or understood her.

She wished Frank were there. She could have talked to him instead of carrying on this awkward and frustrating monologue. Besides, she needed his physical help.

When she turned in at her driveway, there were lights on in the big house. She wondered whether Gigi had ever turned up, and where she had been. She wondered why Debra had gotten into such a swivet. A fifteen-year-old was no baby. Probably Debra felt guilty because she didn't really like the girl. Gigi was convinced that she didn't.

When they reached their own house, Billy sat still until she opened the door to help him out. Then his eyes widened as though in alarm.

"Look, honey, we're home now," she said. "Let me get the door unlocked and then I'll rush you right inside. See, there's only one step. I can manage that."

The wind whipped her coat as she went to open the door. She could not get the car any closer, but at least the rain was only a sprinkle now. The storm had flattened some of her flowers, but she thought they would probably pick up once it was over.

At least she had Billy. That was the most important thing of all. She would do everything she could to get him back to normal. She would *will* it. Just because he tried to kill himself didn't mean he should be punished forever.

She unfolded the wheelchair and reached for him. He grabbed her shoulder to support himself. It was a gratifying moment of closeness, even though he had not intended it that way.

They made a quick dash along the walk and then were inside, out of the punishing wind. She knew exactly what Frank would have said. He would have told her she was insane not to wait until tomorrow. It made her glad he had not come after all.

"See? Don't you like it?" she said. "I put a new cover on the sofa and everything's arranged differently. Of course, it's smaller. And here's the television over here."

It was strange and yet familiar. She did not know which would please him more. Or less. She removed the nylon windbreaker he had worn. His pants were sprinkled with drops of rain, but they would soon dry.

"Do you want the television on?" she asked.

He shook his head, then changed his mind and nodded. At least he could manage yes and no. She turned him to face it and placed the remote control in his hand. Then she went to bake the lasagna.

When dinner was ready, she tried to call Frank again. Ann, one of the real estate salespeople, told her Frank had left almost an hour ago.

So he wasn't coming home, Enid thought bitterly. There was no point in combing through the McCoys in the county phone book. They had probably gone to a motel anyway. She sighed, and set the table with two places.

Billy needed help with eating. She had known that. She had often helped him at the nursing home. His hands did not coordinate well and he had trouble lifting his arms.

But he would get there. She would see to that, no matter what it took. She kept up an inane chatter while they ate, talking about the neighborhood, the new tenants, the office. Much of it she had already told him. She began to wish she had left the television on to distract them both, but it was newstime and that was always grim.

Damn it, Frank, she thought as she cleared the table. You'll have to face it someday. You'll have to get used to him.

Unless Frank chose to move out and live with his mistress. Enid would not have put it past him.

The evening was long and strangely illuminated with a yellowish glow. After a while the rain stopped entirely, but the wind still blew. It blew away some of the overcast. From time to time there was a glimmer of sunshine, and then it would cloud again.

Billy seemed morose and wouldn't look at her. He kept his eyes on the television screen. She was surprised he hadn't had his fill of television at the nursing home.

"Isn't it nice that your room's right next to the living room," she said. "We can push the TV in there so you can watch in bed, if you want to."

The only trouble was that both rooms looked out at their old house, which perhaps he did not want to see. She had no idea how he felt about it, and he had certainly been opposed to coming home.

She washed the dishes and listened to the restless sound of changing channels. He was not really watching. That bothered her.

The whole thing bothered her. He did not want to be home. He had no use for her. Dr. Longwort had been right. They were all right. She wasn't good for him, her own son.

She forced back tears. How come people like Lois had it so easy? And Hazel Jorgenson, despite her complaints of doing it alone. Seemingly without effort, they raised successful, loving children. It was no wonder they were convinced that Enid must have done something wrong.

She went into the living room, not wanting to intrude, but feeling that it would be worse to ignore Billy altogether.

He was intent upon a game show, his face still hard. From time to time he raised his head and looked out of the window at the old house.

She wondered what he was thinking. Maybe nothing. Eyes were often drawn to windows, and from that one there was not much choice of view.

He gave a start. She looked and saw the little Gillis boy

prancing through wet grass. They could not see much with all the bushes in the way, but he was evidently having an explosion of energy after being housebound all afternoon.

Billy turned to her, his face working.

"What is it, hon?" she asked.

He tried to lift his arm. He kept turning back to the window. His face became contorted. He needed to tell her something, and he couldn't.

"That's just the little kid who lives there now," she said. "Our tenants' kid. I don't know what he's doing outside, but it's okay. His mother never lets him alone for long."

She had no sooner finished speaking when Debra flew across the grass and scooped him up. The child stiffened, trying to slither out of her arms. He kicked and flailed as she carried him inside. At least she hadn't let him get his way that time, but he was clearly a spoiled brat, as Gigi said.

Billy rocked back and forth, shaking his head.

"What's wrong, sweetie? What is it?"

He couldn't tell her. It was the sight of that little boy that had set him off.

Then she remembered Dr. Longwort's interest in the child found dead on the beach.

It had not been just a passing comment. He had tried to make something of it. Something in a context that included Billy.

It wasn't true. The doctor was crazy. They all were, all bug doctors, as crazy as their patients.

Her throat grew so tight she could scarcely breathe. She felt lightheaded and went to sit down on her bed. Alone.

It was an accident. The child's neck was broken by pounding surf. Stupid children would always go near the water. The Gillis boy yammered constantly about water.

An accident. Of course it was an accident.

CHAPTER 15

Kurt had called earlier in the evening. They were having another meeting that night, he said.

Debra did not believe him. It upset her so that she blew up at Drew when he bolted out the door. He howled with rage as she brought him inside, and she was immediately sorry. He had only wanted to have fun, and she had made him cry. Now that, in turn, was making her cry.

Gigi, who had come out of her room only long enough to survey the table, said, "I don't want any dinner."

Debra sniffled. "That's all right with me."

Gigi stared, then burst out, "What's *wrong* with you? Why don't you have the guts to stand up for yourself?"

Debra sobbed, and Gigi went back to her room, slamming the door. Only after she was gone did Debra realize that Gigi probably thought she was crying about Kurt.

That was not the direct reason. She was too used to Kurt to cry about it anymore. Except when it caused her to be cruel to Drew.

"I'm sorry, honey," she wept. "I was just scared when you went out by yourself. You should wait for Mommy."

Most of their dinner ended up in the refrigerator. She wondered if it could be the barometric pressure that made them all so moody. Ions and things. They had already waited a long time for Kurt, and still they were not hungry.

She stood at the sink, watching the night fall. She saw the flickering of a television picture in the Mauls' little house.

When the last dish was washed, Gigi came out of her room and opened the refrigerator.

"Help yourself," Debra said dully. "Just clean up afterward, please."

Gigi took out the orange juice container and poured herself a glass. Debra wondered how long a person could survive on nothing but orange juice.

"Where were you all day?" she asked.

"Nowhere," Gigi replied.

"All right. As long as you're okay."

"Why wouldn't I be okay?"

Of course Gigi hated it when she pried. And it didn't really matter now. But this secretiveness was bothersome. Somebody had to care what happened to the girl, and her father was never around.

Debra took Drew upstairs and put him to bed. When she went back down, the kitchen light was still on. Groaning at Gigi's carelessness, she went to turn it off and found her stepdaughter at the table, staring into space.

Gigi said, "You know Billy Maul?"

"What about him?" Debra asked.

"He's home now. Right over there in that house. I saw her bringing him in. It was in the middle of the storm, with everything blowing around. She just couldn't wait to get him home. Couldn't even wait till the storm ended."

Debra felt a pang of sympathy for the woman.

"I can't blame her. He's her son. I'd probably feel the same way if it were Drew."

"Why? Do people feel differently about sons?"

"Not necessarily. I probably should have said 'child.' It's just that for her, and for me, and even for Todd's mother, that's what we have."

"Hm." Gigi was silent for a moment. Then she said, "I'd keep an eye on Drew, if I were you."

"I always keep an eye on Drew."

"Todd used to be a pretty good friend of Billy's, you know that?" Gigi continued.

"And?"

"Once he saw Billy . . . Oh, never mind. I don't want to scare you."

"Maybe it's something I should know," Debra said.

"No, you'd only worry. Just keep an eye on Drew, that's all."

"Gigi, I worry anyway. It's my nature. And if there's something special I should watch for, I want to know."

"You're sure? Well, anyway . . . Okay, first I guess I have to tell you that Todd does drugs sometimes."

"I'm not terribly surprised," said Debra.

"You're not? How come?"

"A lot of people do, for some reason. And one time I thought you seemed a little high yourself."

"You thought *I* was high?"

"Well—spaced out, or something."

"I wasn't any of those things, Debra. You were wrong. And you'd better listen to me."

"All right, if you say so." Debra felt abashed. "What were you saying about Billy Maul?"

Gigi, still displeased, exhaled indignantly, then went on with her story.

"Well, Todd isn't the only one who used to do drugs."

"Do you mean Billy did them, too?" Debra asked. "That doesn't surprise me, either. Maybe it had something to do with his suicide attempt."

"No, I'm just about to tell you. At least what Todd thought it might be."

"And that was?" Debra tried to stay calm. If Gigi knew how anxious she was, she might draw this out forever.

"Okay, sometimes Todd used to see Billy going around with that little kid. You know the one that died?"

"Yes, you said Billy used to baby-sit him."

"I did? But this wasn't baby-sitting. Todd said Billy would take him out and buy him ice cream and candy."

"Maybe he likes little children," Debra said.

"Exactly! Or whatever. Todd didn't say. Anyhow, one day Todd was driving down Angel Road and he passed that place where the grave is?"

Debra nodded. She didn't like where this seemed to be leading.

"He saw Billy there," Gigi went on. "He saw him with something on the ground that looked like a bundle of clothes. Todd slowed the car to ask what he was doing. You know, just sort of friendly. Then he saw Billy had a shovel in his hand. And when Todd slowed the car, Billy grabbed this thing that was on the ground and ran off into the trees."

"If Billy was doing something furtive," Debra said, "why would he be doing it right there by the road in broad daylight?"

"I didn't say it was daylight, did I? It was night. And he was back in the trees, not right out in the open. Todd just noticed because he knew Billy. And he knew he was kind of strange."

"But—" Debra did not know why she argued. She didn't want to believe it. "There are houses right across the street, and on either side of that grave area."

"Yes, but it was *dark*. And he could have gotten away with it if Todd didn't see him and slow the car."

"Could have gotten away with what?" Debra asked obtusely.

"God, you're slow," Gigi cried. "That was back in January. And the next day the kid's body was found on the beach. And a little after that, Billy shot himself. So what more do you want me to say?"

"That's probably enough." Debra held herself tightly and stared out of the window at the Mauls' house.

"Well, he's in a wheelchair anyway," Gigi said, "so I guess there's not much you have to worry about. Did I scare you?"

Debra turned from the window. "Do you mean you made it all up?"

"No, it's true! Everything I said is true, unless Todd made it up. But I don't think he would. It bothered him, you know? Because Billy used to be his friend. Anyway, that was what he saw. Maybe it didn't mean anything. Maybe Billy was trying to bury a dead raccoon, or something. But then why the big deal about hiding it?"

"Wouldn't the ground have been frozen last January?" Debra asked.

Gigi groaned. "I'm just telling you what Todd told me. Maybe Billy was planning to use dynamite, I don't know."

"That's very likely. But thank you. I think I'll lock the doors. Except it's nice to have air." Debra examined the screen door and found that it, too, had a lock.

"How's Dad going to get in when he comes home?" Gigi asked. "We don't have keys for the screen doors."

"He can ring," said Debra. "I'll be here."

She hoped he would not be too late. She wanted to tell him what Gigi had said. Maybe they could find another place to live. How would they explain to the Mauls if they wanted to break the lease? Would Kurt agree to try it?

She thought of the trauma of moving again. And there were not that many houses available for rental. Maybe if the Mauls knew the truth about Billy—although who would tell them?—maybe they wouldn't bring him home anymore.

Would they believe it?

Would I, Debra wondered, if somebody said bad things about Drew?

She could not imagine Drew as anything but a two-year-old. She could not imagine any strangeness or dark evil about him. Instead she saw him as a bundle of clothes in a grassy place where there was a grave . . .

No, no, no.

They would go back to Long Island. If Kurt did not agree, she would take Drew and go live with her parents.

As she locked the front door and checked the downstairs windows to be sure the screens were all latched from the inside, she heard Gigi's door close. She hoped Gigi would spend the rest of the evening holed up in her room.

It seemed very quiet without Kurt. She should have been used to it. He had often taught evening classes, or had various meetings and consultations. Or so he said.

Perhaps it was the house that bothered her. It was so large, with too many dark corners. She turned on another lamp across the room, next to the chair where Kurt would have been sitting if he were there. If he weren't in his study. She tried to pretend he was upstairs, but all she felt was the emptiness.

Gigi's radio blared suddenly and then stopped. She was glad Gigi had had the sense to turn it down.

A sound outside made her jump. She hoped it was Kurt, but she hadn't heard his car or seen its headlights. Fearfully she got up and checked both doors. She unlatched the screen doors and closed the primary ones. Kurt could use his key to get in.

She looked out of the kitchen window. In the Mauls' living room, the television light still glowed.

She heard Gigi's radio again as the door opened and closed. She saw Gigi walk across the kitchen in an old shirt of Kurt's. Her legs were bare and she carried something under her arm.

Her voice came angrily from the back entryway. "What the hell did you do with this door?"

"I locked it." Debra jumped up and went to her. "Please keep your voice down. I don't want Drew to wake up."

Gigi was wrestling with the door.

"Just turn that little knob," Debra told her. "It's a Yale lock." The shirt flapped open. Under it Gigi wore her black bikini.

"Where are you going?" Debra asked.

"Out."

"Wait." She seized the girl's arm. "You can't go out like that."

"Like what? What do you want me to wear? Do you want me to put on my jeans and a heavy wool sweater? For swimming? How about leg warmers?"

"You can't go swimming! It's nighttime."

Gigi's face was set, her jaw squared.

"So it's nighttime," she retorted. "The water's still there, isn't it?"

Debra tightened her grip. "Did you take something? Are you on a drug?"

Gigi giggled. "Me? What are you talking about?"

"You're acting very strange. And I don't care if the water's still there. It's dangerous now. The waves are a mile high after that storm and there aren't any lifeguards."

"So? You think I can't handle it? A little wave?"

"That's what I mean, Gigi. You're drugged. Your judgment is—"

Gigi laughed again and pulled free of Debra's hand. "That's

all you know. I bet you'd be scared to go out."

"I certainly would be."

"What if somebody was drowning? What if Drew was out there?"

"Gigi, no!"

"I'm not afraid of it," Gigi sneered. "That's the kind of stuff I wanted. Wet and wild. And I didn't get my chance today with the rain."

"You can't!" cried Debra. "Don't trust yourself now. You don't know what you're doing."

Oh, please, Kurt. Come home.

"Are you going to stop me?" Gigi danced backward, daring her. For a moment Debra thought she wanted to be stopped, but she didn't.

"Look at yourself!" Debra cried. "You're crazy. You think you're all right, but you're crazy. Your father's going to come home and—"

"Yeah? Well, I won't be here." Gigi danced out into the night.

Debra clutched at the door. What had the girl taken? She had never seen anything like it before.

"Come back here!" she shouted.

It was too late. And she couldn't leave Drew.

Call the police? Would they care? Would they have the power to intervene? Or were Gigi's civil rights protected to the extent that she was allowed to kill herself?

Debra remembered those raging waves, tossing gray and yellow before the sun went down. She had watched them from an upstairs window. She had gotten a pair of binoculars because they were so dramatic.

Gigi couldn't have meant it. She was going to meet Todd.

But she had been wearing a swimsuit and carrying a towel.

Debra picked up the telephone and called Kurt's office. Fear ran through her, making her tremble. She heard the ringing. On and on.

Damn it, Kurt. It's your own daughter.

She called the college's main number. No one answered. It was only an office, and they were all closed.

She called the police. They didn't understand what she was talking about.

"Do you mean the kid's out there now?" they asked. "It's running pretty high after the storm."

"That's what I mean!" Debra cried. "She's taken some drug and it made her crazy and I can't leave home. I have a little child asleep. Isn't there anything you can do?"

"We'll have one of our cars look out for her," they said.

"But she's at the beach. The street doesn't go right by there because of the park. What happens if they don't see her? Are you going to let her drown?"

"If she's there, we'll see her," they answered calmly. "There aren't too many people swimming right now."

"But she's on something," Debra pleaded again. "She doesn't know what she's doing. She doesn't understand."

"We'll watch for her," they repeated.

It was not enough.

She started up the stairs to be sure Drew was still sleeping, then remembered she had forgotten to relock the door.

She hurried down and locked it. Then up again.

He was asleep, his thumb in his mouth. Gently she removed the thumb. He murmured but did not wake.

She put on sneakers to be able to run faster, and slipped a housekey into the pocket of her jeans.

She agonized for a moment, thinking of Drew. What if he woke? What if he went downstairs and played with the stove?

She wished there were a key to his room, but there wasn't.

She propped a chair under the knob of his door. She had put locks on his windows so he couldn't open them wide.

Again she hesitated. There was no way she could leave him. Not for any reason.

She opened the door as silently as possible and looked once more. He took a deep sighing breath and kicked his leg, knocking the sheet half off. She hoped he wasn't waking. Fearful of disturbing him further if she tried to adjust his covers, she closed the door and replaced the chair.

She went out the front door, locking it carefully. The wind assaulted her, but it was not a cold wind. She hurried down the walk and out to the street.

It was almost deserted. There were lights on in other houses, but very few people were about. Bits of trash blew high in the wind.

She looked up at the sky. A cloud glowed faintly where the moon was. Dark clouds scudded over lighter ones. She crossed the avenue and hurried on.

A woman, her hair blowing wildly, walked her dog. Farther along, a newspaper had given way to the wind and lay scattered on someone's lawn. How could Gigi be so crazy as to swim in that weather? How could anyone want to swim at night, when they couldn't see what was in the water?

The paths through the park were brightly lit to discourage mischief. No one was there. Everyone had the sense to stay home when a branch might come crashing down at any moment.

Even from there, she could see how high the waves were. Towering, hurling themselves at the shore. No one could even approach that water, much less swim in it. She felt relieved. Gigi must have changed her mind.

The lifeguard's tower had blown over. The tide was high, lashing at the beach. She looked up and down the lonely stretch. There was no sign of Gigi.

Then she saw something flapping in the middle of the sand. It was weighted down by a dark shape. A pair of shoes.

Gigi's shirt and towel.

CHAPTER 16

Finally Billy was in bed. He had not given her much trouble about that, but Enid still wondered at his reaction to seeing the Gillis boy.

He had never done that before. Never seemed so agitated at the sight of a little child. But it couldn't really mean anything. She was too influenced by that crazy doctor and his sinister but obvious suspicions.

Frank hadn't come home yet. It was just as well. She couldn't tell Frank about that, and she couldn't seem to think of anything else. Only Billy.

He hated her. That was clear. He hadn't wanted to come home with her. She was bad for him and he knew it.

They had been right all along. Frank and all the others. She had ruined her own child's life.

She felt sick, hating herself. If only she could care for Billy now and make it up to him—but he didn't want that. He wanted nothing to do with her.

No one wanted her. Not even Frank.

A lump of sadness filled her throat. It grew, weighing her down until it crushed her entire being. The only answer was annihilation.

She fought against it. This was her home. She belonged here. What would happen to the flowers?

Still, it was better to destroy herself than Billy. If he was a monster, she must have made him what he was. If he was only a victim, she had done that, too. Either way, it was more than she could live with.

Restlessly she wandered from room to room. Billy had proven them all right. She felt a wave of anger, and then it was gone. It was not Billy's fault, but hers.

She looked out of the window at her car. All she could see was a faint gleam behind a blowing lilac bush. She could get into it and turn on the engine. But would it work in the open like that? People who tried it usually did so in a closed garage, and she had no garage.

She searched the bathroom. Frank used an electric shaver. She had nothing but disposable razors herself, and the blades were small. She would have to crack the plastic to get one out, and then it would be difficult to grip. She had a few double-edged blades she had saved for scraping paint, but they were no longer sharp.

A kitchen knife, perhaps. She looked through them all, trying to choose.

A broken bottle. She could break a bottle and use the jagged edge. But the car seemed cleaner. Less painful.

Frank would send Billy back to the nursing home. It was where he wanted to be. And maybe, in her absence, Frank would visit him sometimes. She thought how bleak it would be for Billy without her caring, and then remembered that her caring was bad for him. She must stop thinking of that. She had been wrong from the start. Now she needed to do this thing for herself.

Hazel had a garage, and it was often left open. Usually they parked outside. She would drive past and see if she could get into it. If not, she would go to Frank's parking lot. No one would be there at night, and she could sit under the tree that connected Frank's lot and the bank.

Out of habit, she took her purse. She checked to be sure the gas jets were off. In spite of everything, she did not want to harm Billy.

She started toward the door. She would not think any longer of what she was doing, but just do it.

A shout came from Billy's room.

She stopped and listened.

It *was* a shout. He had made a vocal sound. Not a real word, but he had used his voice. It was the first time since February.

Could he possibly have guessed her thoughts?

She found him outside his room, clutching the wall. He was trying to move along it. He reached the door of the master bedroom.

"Dud!" he cried in a hoarse voice. "Dud!"

"Billy, what is it? Dad's not here." She reached out to help him.

He backed against the wall. He did not want her to touch him.

"Dud!" he said again.

"But Dad's not here. What do you want? Let me help you."

Maybe he was embarrassed to have her care for him intimately. Or maybe he preferred Frank to her. Maybe Frank's coldness was better than too much caring. It left him freer.

"Dud!" Billy's body jerked in an effort to make her understand.

"I don't know what you want," she said.

"Dud! Dud!" He looked back toward his own room.

"Dad should be here soon. He had to work late."

What if Frank stayed away all night with that girl?

Billy clawed at the wall.

"Do you want to use the bathroom?" she asked.

Violently he shook his head.

"Do you want to go back to bed? Come, let's get you back in bed."

She tried to take his arm. He pulled away. Lurching around her, he staggered into the living room. He seemed to be trying to reach the door.

"Billy!" she cried. "Don't go out there!"

She blocked his way. "What is it you want, honey? Tell me. Do you want to go back to the nursing home? Do you really want to?"

He paused, seeming confused. His head dropped forward. She caught him to keep him from falling.

Again he pulled away from her. He moved toward the kitchen. The back door?

No, it was the telephone. He seized it, knocking it off the countertop.

"I don't know what you want," she cried helplessly.

He could not bend over to pick up the phone without losing his balance. She retrieved it and held it out to him. He shook his head in frustration.

"Do you want to call Dad?" she asked.

He couldn't use the phone. They both knew it. She replaced it on the counter as he gestured wildly toward the front door.

Again he shook his head. He tore at his hair. He pointed toward the door.

"But it's windy out there," she said. If Billy felt stupid and helpless, so did she.

He stamped his foot. "Dud!" he cried again and again.

"Dad will be home later. Is there something you want to tell Dad?"

He shook his head. His face was anguished. Again he pointed to the door.

He raised his arms and tried to show her in pantomime. His body refused to obey. The aphasia that would not let him use words also kept him from expressing his thoughts with action.

Enid caught him as he rushed toward the back door.

He did not try to open it. He pointed toward the street. Angel Road. He hesitated, as though trying to think. Then he pointed to the left.

"Dud!" he shouted. "Dud! Dud!"

"But I told you, Dad's—"

His head wagged back and forth. He seized her arm and shook it. "Dud!" he cried, pointing up the street.

"Oh . . ." Her mind seemed to clear. She had put too much emphasis on her own interpretation. "Do you mean Todd? Is that what you mean?"

His eyes widened as though a light had been turned on. He nodded so vigorously that it shook his whole body.

"Do you want to see Todd?" she asked.

The nodding turned to a negative answer. His upper torso swung back and forth. Briefly she wondered if the aphasia let him correctly distinguish between yes and no. Was he really saying what he meant?

"You don't want to see Todd?"

Another wholehearted shake.

"Then I don't know what you want," she said.

He lumbered over to the phone. He lifted the receiver and slammed it down.

"You want to call Todd?"

NO. Again he tore at his hair.

"Then what is it you want, sweetie? I don't understand."

He went into a frenzy of motion, pointing toward the living room. The front door. He placed his hand near the floor. He took a step forward and lurched into the dinette table. She caught him before he could fall.

He jerked away from her. He waved toward the living room.

"You don't want to see Todd," she tried again.

He shook his head.

"You don't want to call him."

Another, very definite shake.

"You don't want . . . I don't know."

Again and again he flung his arm at the living room. He pointed to his head.

"Does it hurt?" she asked.

NO. That was not what he meant. She clutched at her own head, trying to think.

"Dud!" he cried. "Dud!"

"Yes, I know. Todd." What could he want with Todd, if he did not want to see him or call him?

"Wait a minute, Billy. Wait. Let's both take it easy. You sit here."

She pushed him into a dinette chair. Puzzled and docile, he sat still. She took a seat on the other side of the table so that she faced him over a corner.

"We're going to do this logically," she said. "We're going to play it like Twenty Questions. Remember?"

He stared at her, waiting. Then he nodded. He understood.

But he still seemed agitated. Whatever it was, it was something urgent. Something very important.

"It's about Todd," she began. "You want to tell me something about Todd."

He nodded yes.

"But you don't want to see him."

No, he did not.

"Something you remembered about Todd?"

He shook his head.

She tried to think back to how it had begun.

He had come out of his room, calling the word that proved to be Todd's name. His windows faced the other house, where the Gillises lived.

"You saw Todd?" she asked. "Just now?"

A violent yes.

"You saw Todd over there? Where we used to live?"

Another yes. His face lit up with excited agreement.

"He goes there sometimes," she explained. "He goes to see the girl who lives there now."

Billy stopped her. That was not it. He pounded the table.

"I don't understand," she said.

He pounded again. "Dud!"

"Todd . . . did something?"

He nodded. Yes. He pointed to his head.

"Todd did something to you? Just now?"

No. No. She was lost again.

He jabbed a finger toward his head. Exactly where the bullet had gone.

"Todd—"

She could not believe what she was thinking.

"Do you mean . . . it was Todd? Do you mean he shot you? It was *Todd* who shot you?"

Yes! Yes!

She did not believe it.

"Billy, are you sure?"

YES.

"Do you mean—last winter—when you got hurt—it was *Todd* who did it? Todd did that to you?"

Yes! Yes! Yes!

She half rose from her chair. She wanted to hug him. To cry. It was not suicide. He hadn't shot himself. It was murder.

Murder.

"Are you sure?"

He pounded on the table.

"Billy, I believe you. Oh, sweetie." Her arms went around him. Her boy.

He struggled away from her.

"What is it, dear?" She should not have seemed so pleased. "I'm just glad you didn't do it to yourself, but I'm not glad it happened. I'll call the police."

He put his hand over the phone.

"You don't want me to call? Then what is it? What do you want?"

He pointed toward the living room.

"Todd's out there?"

He hesitated. She was almost right.

He put his hand near the floor. He moved his feet, one step forward.

"I don't know what you mean," she said.

In despair he clutched at his head and rocked back and forth.

He couldn't make her understand.

CHAPTER 17

Again and again Debra called into the wind. Nothing was out there but dark, wild water.

It was a trap. A trap to lure her to death.

But there were the clothes. Where had Gigi gone in only her bikini? Debra shivered.

Or did she have an accomplice? Had Todd met her with another shirt? And some shoes? Not Todd, who had been so polite and pleasant.

Was it Kurt? Had he gotten Gigi to help him?

She screamed again. Called Gigi's name.

Then she saw it.

The moon had glimmered. She saw Gigi's head. Her golden hair. Flailing arms.

A mirage. The moon had played tricks.

"Gigi!" she cried.

It was a trick.

She pulled off her sneakers. No one could get out there.

Again she saw the hair.

"Gigi, come back! I'll help you!"

Her voice was feeble in the wind and crashing waves. And Gigi could not come back. She was drowning.

Debra stepped to the edge of the water. It lashed at her feet. It swirled around her ankles and began to drag at her.

She turned her shoulder against the waves. They would crush her. She could not get out there. But Gigi was drowning.

She stopped trying to think and worked by instinct. There was no way she could fight the breakers. She would have to slip in between them. With exquisite timing, of which she was barely aware, she got herself beyond the curling crests. But the mountainous swells of water carried her back toward the shore. They would smash her. She paddled furiously against them.

Once more the moon came out. She could see Gigi, closer than she had thought. Gigi's face was expressionless and she swam with all her strength to keep afloat. Water washed into her mouth. She spat it out. She saw Debra coming and briefly closed her eyes.

Debra fought the ocean's force. She couldn't move. Yet she had swum out this far. Swum through the breakers. It was shallow here, but with each rolling wave she was lifted off her feet and thrown back toward the beach.

Again she struggled outward. She could almost touch Gigi. Again they were washed apart.

The water blinded her. It filled her mouth. She threw herself forward and touched the flowing hair.

Gigi's arms leaped at her. They wrapped around Debra's neck and pushed her under the water.

Shocked, Debra had been caught without air. She forced herself not to breathe. She pounded and kicked at the weight that held her down. She struggled for the surface but couldn't reach it.

She had to force her own body not to breathe. Fight her way out of the water.

She grasped at Gigi's arms and tried to pry them off. Tried to push Gigi under. The arms were slippery. She couldn't hold.

Debra kicked again. Her head broke the surface. She saw the moon. She opened her mouth and gulped in air.

Gigi's foot struck her belly. Debra fell back and the water closed over her.

She was dying. She would die and wash ashore.

She thought of Drew. It was all she had. Drew.

She was all *he* had.

The water stung her nose. Again she gulped air. She thought how easy to die, but it was not that easy. Something made her want to live.

To see Drew again. Just once.

She saw him in the moon. The moon's face. It was Drew.

Left asleep. He could not get out of his room.

She sank again. There was something in her hand. Gigi's hair.

Again she rose to the surface. Again the moon shone.

But it wasn't Drew. He was home in bed. She kicked toward the shore.

A wave lifted her, tossed her, then washed her back out toward the sea.

CHAPTER 18

Debra heard a voice. Something dragged at her.

Gigi's hand. Feebly she tried to fight it off.

"Take it easy," said the voice.

She was lifted by her arms and dragged over hard sand. She coughed. Her nose and mouth still burned from salt water.

The voice asked, "You okay?" It was a man's voice. "I've got the other girl. She's not breathing."

Debra tried to speak. Her throat burned. She fell back on the sand.

"As soon as you can," the man told her, "you'd better go for help. I can't leave her. I'm trying to make her breathe."

Debra lay on the sand and gasped for air. After a while she tried to sit up.

"Take it easy," said the man. "I'll do what I can."

She didn't know what he was doing. She heard him grunt and pound on something. She lay where she was and took one breath after another.

What did I do? she wondered.

Gigi. Had fought her off. Tried to drown them both.

Debra opened her mouth to speak. She had no voice. She tried to clear her throat and began to cough.

She was still full of water. Sodden and drowned.

But she was out in the air. She could breathe, with each breath tearing through her.

The coughing subsided and she rested her head again.

She remembered Drew. Alone in the house.

"Drew," she whispered, and tried to sit up.

A few feet away she saw a dark shape. A man. He was bending over something on the sand. She recognized Gigi's golden hair.

"I have to . . . get—" Debra tried to say. Her voice was silent.

The man turned to look at her.

"Soon as you're okay," he said, and bent over Gigi again. "Better go for help. Can't get her breathing."

"My boy," Debra whispered.

"You okay?"

He had little time to talk. He was busy trying to pump breath into Gigi's lungs.

"Have to . . . have to get—" she gasped, and rose to her knees.

Drew. Alone.

Why didn't Kurt come? He was busy with his woman.

It was her fault. Too wrapped up in Drew.

Because Kurt didn't want her.

She had to do it alone. Even save Kurt's child.

"Crazy," she whispered.

"What did you folks do?" asked the man, and pumped another breath. "Fall off a boat?"

"Crazy," she tried to tell him. "Crazy. Drug."

What drug would make Gigi act like that? Debra couldn't

think. She managed to stand up. A gust of wind pushed her down.

"Better go for help," the man told her again. "Go to one of those houses over there. Tell them to call an ambulance."

She finally realized what he was saying. Gigi wasn't breathing. She was dead.

I tried, Debra thought. *I tried.*

But Drew was alive. She had to get to him.

Again she struggled to stand. This time she was prepared for the wind and braced herself against it.

"Tell them to call an ambulance," the man reminded her. He turned back to Gigi. "Hey! Young lady!"

Debra thought she heard a cough. She couldn't be sure. The wind drowned out everything.

She was in the park before she remembered her shoes.

There was no time to go back. Her feet were numb anyway. But when she stepped on a pebble, the pain shot through her.

She thought of Drew and kept going.

And Gigi. She hated Gigi. Why had she done it?

Gigi was dead.

Yet there was that faint sound, like a cough. Her hatred was mixed with a feeling of responsibility. Gigi mustn't die!

She had never before admitted that she hated Gigi.

She left the park and crossed the first street. There were houses. Tell them to call an ambulance.

Her own house was two more blocks. She felt in her pocket. The key was still there. A deep, tight pocket.

She tried to run. To get home. Her legs were slow and heavy. But if she were home, she would have to call the ambulance herself, and she couldn't talk.

The first house on the corner was dark. She started up Angel Road.

The next had lights. Through an open window she heard

television. Loud. She rang the bell.

She pounded on the door.

They couldn't hear her. She turned away.

The door opened.

It was a teenage boy, Oriental, in shorts. He stared at her with faint alarm. She looked terrible. Drowned.

"Call an ambulance," she wheezed.

He continued to stare. "Are you okay?"

"Not me." She still could not talk. "Accident. On the beach. Girl drowned. Call an ambulance. Please. It's right . . . right down there." Debra pointed toward the park.

"Angel Road?" asked the boy.

She nodded and pointed again.

"Come on in." He held the door wider. She heard laughter.

"Can't." She shook her head. "Got to go. Please call. Right now. Thanks."

"Yeah. Sure." He looked at her as though not quite sure. She backed away and he closed the door.

She hurried on. He probably thought she was crazy. But she had obviously been in the water. Would he call? She thought of trying another house.

From home. She had to reach home. The number would be in the phone book.

A car passed by. The driver looked at her, with her wet clothes and bare feet, and didn't stop. At the next intersection she waited for two cars before she could cross. No one stopped to ask what was wrong. Maybe they didn't see her. Too busy. Or they didn't care.

Another block. She was home. She ran up the walk. A crumbling piece of concrete caught her foot. She cried out.

She limped up the steps and across the porch. She was home. The key in her hand.

Should have left a light on. She couldn't see the keyhole.

She groped for it with her other hand. She was shaking. Why wasn't Kurt there?

The key worked hard. She had to hold the latch steady. An old-fashioned door with a latch instead of a knob.

Finally it turned. She slipped inside, then closed and locked the door.

Still quiet. She hurried upstairs, saw that the chair was still in place outside his door, then went back to the kitchen.

On the inside cover of the phone book were numbers for police, ambulance, fire. Again and again she cleared her throat as she dialed.

A man answered. Debra could barely talk. There was only a thin thread of vocal sound in all the wheeze.

"Send an ambulance," she managed to say. "The beach. Foot of Angel Road. A girl drowned."

"Yeah, okay," said the man. "We already got a call on that. Thanks."

"Thank you." She was grateful to the boy. He had not known what to make of her, but he called.

She hung up the phone and coughed again to clear her throat. She went into the downstairs bathroom and looked at herself in the mirror, wondering what the boy had seen.

It was not as bad as she thought. Her hair was wet and mussed. Her shirt clung tightly, showing the outline of her bra. She reached for Gigi's towel to dry her hair, but could not bring herself to touch it.

She wondered if Gigi was really dead. What would happen? How would Kurt ever understand?

She went upstairs to use her own towel, then combed her hair so she wouldn't frighten Drew if he happened to wake.

She needed to see him. Needed to know that he, at least, was safe. The sight of him would make her safe, too. She slipped the chair out from under the knob and pushed it aside.

She turned the knob, trying not to make a sound.

A stream of light from the hallway fell onto his bed, showing a rumpled sheet. He had kicked it off, she remembered. She did not see his legs.

She went into the room and stared at his bed, willing herself to see him there.

The bed was empty.

She felt a chill as she approached it. An empty bed. It couldn't be. She blinked and tried to clear the water from her eyes.

"Drew?"

She turned on the light. How could he have gotten out? If he had, he would not have replaced the chair. She looked under the bed. In the closet. In his toy box, although it was too small to conceal him.

The windows. Oh God, the windows.

But he could not have gotten through them. They were open only a few inches and locked so he couldn't open them wider.

She struggled with the sash, trying to look and see if he could have fallen. It wouldn't open. Even as she thought about the locks, she had forgotten them.

She released the catch, pushed up the window, and leaned out.

He was not there. No broken body lying on the grass. He couldn't have gotten out.

She sat down on the bed, trembling and sick to her stomach. She called his name again.

She heard nothing but silence.

He was gone.

CHAPTER **19**

Debra raced through the house, turning on lights. Each room. Every closet. The basement, large and empty, with a red carpet on the floor and Kurt's book cartons stacked in one corner. She looked in the unfinished part of the basement. In the clothes dryer.

Gigi's words came back to her.

Disappeared out of his bed at night.

The child who was found on the beach. Dead.

Just before Billy Maul shot himself.

And Todd . . . Todd had said—

She could not remember. But Billy Maul was home now. Gigi had seen him.

Debra shivered. There was no time to change her wet clothes.

She ran out of the house and across the yard. Drew's yard. That happy place. She pounded on the door.

Enid Maul flung it open. She looked distraught and alarmed. Impatient.

Debra cried, "My little boy! He's gone! He was in his bed!"
"What do you want?" asked Enid.
Debra pushed past her.

She could see through an archway into the kitchen. A figure sat at the table. A man. A boy, with light brown hair. Enid's face. He rested heavily on his forearm and watched her.

She clasped her hands and tried to hold herself still.

"My boy. He's gone. I had his door closed tight and now he's gone."

Enid asked, "Did you call the police?"

"No. No . . ." Debra hadn't thought of the police. Because she knew . . .

The man hadn't moved.

"That's your son," she said.

"That's my son," Enid confirmed.

"I want my boy! I want him back."

"Shall I call the police?" Enid started toward the kitchen. Debra saw a telephone on the dinette table, its cord extending into the wall.

She screamed, "What did he do? I want my boy!"

"I don't know what you're talking about," said Enid. "I'll ring the number for you, and you tell them what happened. But you'll have to make sense. And then you be quiet, because Billy's trying to tell me something important."

Billy's face worked. He raised a clumsy arm and pointed toward the living room. He uttered a syllable that sounded like "Dut."

Debra recoiled. He was grotesque. Dangerous. A monster.

Before she could think, before Enid could pick up the phone, the front door opened. A man struggled to close it against the wind. He was big and dark, and when he anchored the door and turned toward them, Debra thought he looked like the man on the beach. The man who had pulled her out of the water.

It had been dark and she was nearly drowned. But when he saw her, he said with some surprise, "Hey, you're here. You feeling okay now? I got the girl breathing. The ambulance took her."

"My little boy's gone," Debra told him. "I went home and he was gone. I had him fastened in his room."

The man's head jerked back. "Yeah?"

Enid raised her voice as though in anger. "She says her kid is missing. I'm calling the police because she's not making sense. And then the two of you shut up. Billy's trying to tell me something important."

She picked up the telephone and punched out a number, then handed the receiver to Debra.

Tearfully Debra spoke, not knowing to whom she was talking.

"My little boy. He's gone. I had him in his room with the door shut and braced. I had to go out. My stepdaughter went crazy. She was going to the beach."

"Your name and address?" asked the voice.

"Gillis." She spelled it for them. "Four forty-five Barton Avenue, the corner of Angel Road. He's only two and a half. His name is Drew."

Enid snatched the phone from her and spoke into it.

"Come to the house in back," she said. "There's two houses. Come to the little one in back. That's where she is, and there's something else going on here, okay?"

She listened for a moment, then hung up.

"You saw Todd out the window, right?" she asked her son.

Billy nodded.

The dark man asked, "What's going on here?" He turned to

Debra. "You're Mrs. Gillis, huh? I'm Frank Maul."

Enid waved him to be quiet.

She said to Billy, "You saw Todd out the window. What was he doing?"

Billy reached down and held his hand above the floor.

"Was he alone?" Enid asked.

He shook his head.

"He had somebody with him?"

Billy nodded yes, and again put his hand near the floor.

"Do you mean it was something small? A child? Is that what you mean?"

Yes again, emphatically.

"Was it the one you saw before, who lives in that house?"

A violent nod.

"You see?" Enid turned triumphantly to Debra. "That's what he was trying to tell me, and you came bursting in like a maniac. He saw it from his bedroom window. He saw Todd with your little boy." She asked Billy, "Were they coming from the house?"

Billy nodded.

"Where did they go?"

He hesitated, his hand poised, as though trying to orient himself. Then he pointed toward the street.

"There now," said Enid. "It was Todd who took your boy."

"Todd?" Debra's voice quavered. She didn't understand.

"It was Todd," Enid repeated. "And Billy was trying to tell me all along, but I didn't know. He wanted to go after Todd. He wanted to call the police, I guess."

"But, Todd—" Debra began.

"You don't know. Billy told me—" Enid spoke to her husband. "Billy said—" Her voice broke. Her eyes filled with tears.

Billy lifted his hand and pointed to his head.

"It was Todd who shot him," Enid cried. "Billy didn't do it, it was Todd!"

"Huh?" said Frank. "Todd? Why?"

The telephone rang. Enid picked it up. She listened briefly, her face growing slack, then set it down.

Frank asked, "What was that?"

"I don't know." She shook her head disbelievingly. "It was somebody. He said— He said, 'When I finish this, I'll be coming for Billy.' Then he hung up."

"What do you mean 'somebody'?" Frank demanded.

"I don't know. It was a man's voice. It didn't sound like Todd."

"Do you think it could have been Todd, maybe disguised?" he asked.

"I guess it could have been. I don't know."

"What the hell—" Frank scowled at his son. "What the hell would Todd want to hurt you for?"

Billy looked blank. He lifted his hands from the table and let them fall.

"He can't tell you," said Enid. "He doesn't have the words."

"I don't get it. It makes no sense to me."

Billy nodded.

Frank eyed him warily. "It does make sense?"

Another affirmative.

Debra moaned. "Kurt. I've got to get my husband."

The Mauls paid no attention to her. She said again, "I've got to get my husband. I have his number at home."

They were still questioning Billy as she went out the door. The wind caught and battered her. She fought her way through it across the yard.

The kitchen door opened without a key. She had forgotten to

lock it when she ran to the Mauls'.

But she had locked it before. How could Todd have gotten in?

Or was it a lie? The Mauls would have a key.

Kurt's number was in her personal book which she kept under the telephone. Her hand shook as she tried to press the digits.

Please be there. Please.

She needed him. The Mauls were against her. It was a lie that they had seen Todd take Drew out of the house. A lie that Todd had been the one to shoot Billy.

Kurt didn't answer. She bit her knuckle, hearing the endless ringing.

Someone would have to pick it up. There must have been someone in that office building.

Not at night. Furiously she threw down the phone.

Headlights flashed past her window and up the driveway to the Mauls' house.

The police. She would have to go back. And hear their lies.

She hurried across the yard, entering the house without knocking. They were all in the living room. All three Mauls and two police officers, a man and a woman. Debra stood shivering, wet and cold. And still barefooted. There had been no time to think of shoes.

"That's the one whose kid is missing," said Enid Maul.

"Are you sure he's not somewhere in the house?" asked the woman, who had short, curly hair and a figure that strained at her uniform.

Debra nodded. "I looked." Her voice had gone hoarse again.

"I told you," said Enid. "Billy saw the kid being taken out of the house."

161

"How do you know what Billy saw?" asked the woman. Billy frowned in dismay.

"We do it like Twenty Questions," Enid explained. "And that's what he saw."

Billy nodded.

Frank Maul introduced Debra by name. The two officers were Sue Ottleson and Ben Feister.

Ottleson was writing in a notebook. "Let's have a description of your kid," she said.

"He's two and a half," Debra began. "He has brown hair, a little lighter than mine, and brown eyes."

His height and weight. She knew everything. His small square hands.

"He had on yellow seersucker pajamas with little ducks. White ducks."

Impassively, Ottleson wrote it all down. Debra might have been describing a stolen car.

Enid turned to Billy. "Was he still wearing those pajamas?"

Billy lifted his shoulders and gave a slow, dazed shake of the head.

"He doesn't know," said Enid. "It was dark."

"You're putting words in his mouth," Frank told her.

"It *was* dark."

Ben Feister asked, "Did it look like it could have been yellow pajamas?"

Billy considered for a moment, then nodded. Debra wondered how much he really understood.

Ottleson telephoned headquarters with the description.

"How did he get in the house?" Ben Feister asked. "Did you know he was there?"

"No, I didn't," said Debra. "I had to—" She looked helplessly at Frank Maul.

"There was a girl drowning at the beach," said Frank.

"My stepdaughter," Debra told them. "She said she was going swimming. In those waves. I thought she was out of her mind. Really. I thought . . . I thought she might have taken a drug. But I couldn't let her go. I went after her."

"Saved her life, too," Frank observed.

"I locked the house," Debra went on. "I braced Drew's door with a chair so he couldn't get out. I just thought of him getting out and wandering. Maybe trying to find me."

"What if the house caught fire?" Ottleson asked, clearly disapproving.

"I thought of that, too. I didn't know what to do. But I knew my stepdaughter didn't know what she was doing. I couldn't let her drown. My husband wasn't home."

"Couldn't you have called for help?"

"I *did*. I called the police. They said they'd watch for her, but that wasn't enough. And nobody was around when I got to the beach."

Enid asked her husband, "How come you were there?"

"I was thinking," he said. Enid looked as though he had slapped her. He went on, not noticing. "I needed to think. It was a lucky thing, too, for those two girls."

Debra appealed to Ben Feister. "Are they really looking for my son? More than they looked for my stepdaughter?"

"They're out now," the man replied. He was tall and well built. Solid. Strong. "We'll go, too, in a minute. You'd better come with us. We can use your help."

"What about Billy?" Enid cried. "There was a phone call. They said they were going to get Billy. I don't know if it was Todd, but what if you miss him and he comes back?"

"I'll be here," said Frank.

Debra caught a flash of gratitude, even love, in Enid's eyes.

Ottleson asked, "Do you know if your stepdaughter did drugs?"

"I think so," said Debra. "I wasn't sure, but I think so. I don't know what would make her act like that. She was all hopped up, full of vinegar, and she didn't have any sense."

"Could be a lot of things," Feister observed. "Could be angel dust. Anybody know what sort of car Jorgenson drives?"

"It's old," said Enid. "Old and dark. A sedan. It's big, too."

Frank said, "Nineteen seventy-eight Buick Regal. Four doors. Black."

"Plate number?"

"That I don't know," he admitted.

"Okay, let's go." Feister ushered his partner and Debra out into the wind.

"What are we going to do?" Debra asked when they were in the car. "Just drive around? Aimlessly?"

"We'll try his home first," said Feister.

They pulled in at the driveway of the Jorgenson house. The garage door stood open and Todd's car was there. Debra felt a leap of hope.

Feister went to the front door and rang the bell. The porch light was on, but the rest of the house was dark. Debra did not see Hazel's car.

"His mother's car isn't here," she told Ottleson.

"Looks like nobody's here," replied the officer.

Feister came back.

"Locked tight," he reported, and radioed to headquarters. He gave the address of the house and asked for a search warrant.

Ottleson seemed surprised. "What for?"

"I've got a hunch," he said.

"Doesn't it take a long time?" asked Debra. Her head swam. What could it mean? Did he think Drew might be in there? Would he be alive?

"A while," Feister answered.

She knew it took hours. It had to be done through the courts, or something like that.

"If his car's here," she said, "doesn't it mean he must be somewhere nearby?"

Feister gave her a look of sympathy as Ottleson backed out of the driveway.

"Could mean anything. Could mean it's going to be harder to find him because we can't look for the car."

"But—are we trying to find my son or Todd Jorgenson?"

"At this point, ma'am, we don't know what we're looking for."

Debra did not need to be told what that meant.

CHAPTER 20

Todd parked his car and looked up at the tree. Its branches waved dangerously in the wind. Except for that, the weather was his ally that night. It kept people indoors and drowned out any sounds he might make.

"Do you see that tree?" he asked the child next to him. "We're going to climb up in that."

"Don't want to climb tree." The child kicked his bare feet. He hadn't even wanted to be waked up. What a temper.

"We're going to climb it," Todd repeated. "You haven't got a choice. But after we finish, and you get that window open for me, I'll buy you some more candy. Here, have another piece." He offered the bag he had brought with him. The boy took a handful of jellybeans and munched them silently.

"Gotta get going," Todd said. "You wait here while I set up. That's some tree, huh? It's no problem with a ladder. Now remember what you do. You go in that window up there. See that window? After we're in the tree, I'll fix the ladder so you can get up there. You go in that window . . . It's not locked, because nobody can get in except a guy your size. Then you go down one flight of stairs to the big window under it. That one there. When you can see me, that's the right window. You turn that gizmo in the middle that unlocks it, and I do the rest. You got that, kid? We'll go over it again in a minute."

He left the child eating jellybeans while he propped his ladder against the tree. This time it was going to work. The other time had been winter and the kid had a coat on. It made him clumsy.

As soon as the ladder was braced, he went back for the child.

"You're a godsend, you know that?" he said. "Now, start climbing. I'll be right behind you. I've got the candy in my pocket, okay? Come on. One foot, then the other foot. You have to get used to it. I'm right here with you."

The rungs were a little far apart for a kid that size. Todd had to boost him up. He hoped it would work better on the next phase of their venture, when the ladder was not so steep. Meanwhile, he kept talking so the child would forget to be afraid.

"Up you go. Right into the tree. You ever been in a tree before? I'll give you some real happy pills after this so you'll forget the whole thing. And more candy, too. You like chocolate?"

The boy whimpered.

"Don't go chicken on me, kid," Todd warned. "I went to a lot of trouble for this and I really need what's in there. I need it a lot more than the bank does. Understand?"

He did not actually believe the child would understand, but hoped his voice would have a calming effect. All he wanted was to get that window unlocked. He was pretty sure he could fix the burglar alarm. But there weren't any alarms on the third floor because nobody could get in that way. Nobody except a very small child.

When it was over, he'd give the kid a little dust and make him forget it. Dust could have that effect. He'd dump him off somewhere, maybe close to home. Nobody would ever know what happened.

There were a few problems, like Billy Maul. Gigi said he couldn't talk. If he ever did, it would be too late anyway.

"Hey, we made it, kid. We're up in the tree. How do you like that?"

"Wanna get down."

"Don't go chicken on me. I told you. Have another jellybean. Now, I'm going to haul this ladder up . . ."

The ladder was aluminum. Easy to lift. And it folded. He could carry it in the trunk of his car. Or rather, his mother's car. He lifted it carefully, trying to keep it from tangling in the branches, and laid it along a sturdy limb that reached up toward the window. When the ladder was braced in the crotch of the tree, he raised the other end until it rested against the windowsill.

"Okay, kid, you're on. Now, remember what you have to do?"

He went through it again. Open the window. Pry it up with this screwdriver and pull it open. Then go down the stairs, right? And unlatch that thing on the big window. Then I'll come in and you can have some more candy. And a little dust. After that, you can go home and see your dad . . .

"Don't wanna go," the boy wailed when Todd showed him how to crawl up the ladder.

"I'll be right here," Todd promised. "Just go up to that window and pry it open. No problem. I'd go with you, but I'm a little heavy. If we're together, we might break the tree. You're doing okay, kid. Remember, as soon as you let me in, I'll give you candy."

"Don't wanna—"

"Uh-uh—" Todd held up a warning finger. "You want to see your mom again? You won't see her if you don't go up there and open those windows."

Maybe a negative was too hard to understand.

"You get that little window open, get the big window open, and I'll take you home to Mommy. Got that? Now, watch your step and hang on tight."

His temper was beginning to fray. He wanted to be long gone by the time Frank Maul came to open his office in the morning. Really long gone. Say in Virginia, on his way to Florida.

"You with me, kid? Go on, take it one step at a time. Remember, there's candy in that bank. Real candy."

There was, too. They kept lollipops by the drive-in window to hand out to people with kids.

He had to cajole a little more and threaten a lot, but finally the boy started up. One rung. A second rung. Todd had been talking so much he forgot to notice how badly the tree was swaying.

"Never mind the wind," he called when the child looked back. "It's not going to hurt you. Just a big lot of air. It's the clouds blowing each other around. Now get up there, okay? You get that open . . ." He dangled the bag of jellybeans.

The boy crawled up another rung. He began to whimper. Kind of young, maybe, but just the right size.

"A little more," Todd called to him.

The child froze.

"Keep going. There's only one way and that's up. You hear me?"

The boy was not moving. Damn it, thought Todd.

A branch of leaves swooped threateningly. The child cowered, his voice rising in a wail.

"Hang on there!" Todd shouted. "Don't let—"

169

The boy lost his grip.

It happened too fast. Damn the leaves. Damn—

Clawing, screaming, tumbling . . .

Todd looked down at the light-colored heap on the ground below. A bundle in an odd, twisted position. He watched to see it move, but nothing happened.

"Shit," he said as he stared at it. "Aw, shit."

CHAPTER 21

The police car cruised along the waterfront in a commercial area of hot dog and hamburger stands, pizzerias, ice-cream parlors, souvenir shops, and video arcades.

Debra leaned forward to the two officers, who were busy talking with each other in the front seat.

"Why would they be here? Why would Todd bring him to a place like this?"

"We have to try everything, ma'am," Feister replied. "We don't know what the fella wanted with him in the first place."

"You got any better ideas?" Ottleson tossed over her shoulder.

It seemed to Debra that it would have been a more secret place. If Todd wanted Drew at all, and had schemed to get him, it would have been for some clandestine reason. Even sex, she admitted, and shook her head to rid herself of the thought.

But where would that secret place be? Ottleson was right. She had no better ideas.

And so they cruised—past the waterfront, onto the main business street, which was nearly deserted at night. The shops were closed, the parking meters standing idle. Dim fluorescent lights glowed in most of the stores. She peered into each one.

There were shoe stores, liquor stores, flower shops, boutiques. A pharmacy and a stationer. She saw FRANK MAUL REALTY, and underneath it, INSURANCE, a low building standing next to a three-story bank. Debra looked, but did not see anything moving. Only bits of trash blowing in the wind.

She wondered where Hazel Jorgenson was. Would Hazel ever believe that her son had taken little Drew?

Again she leaned forward.

"How do you know Billy Maul was telling the truth? He might have done something himself."

"We don't rule that out," said Feister. "Except he didn't look terribly mobile. And so far Jorgenson's whereabouts can't be accounted for."

"Maybe he's at home. Just because he didn't answer the door . . ."

"Can't get in without a search warrant," Feister replied.

"Please try again. What about near the beach? The park?"

"Kind of windy, isn't it?"

"Yes, but—maybe he took drugs, too. My stepdaughter wanted to go out in it."

"We'll give it a try."

Feister said something to his partner and they swung onto Seaside Avenue, which ran along next to the park.

Debra was struck by another idea.

"Could I get into Todd's house? I'm not the police, so you wouldn't have to take responsibility. I'd be willing to break a window or anything."

"We'd have to charge you with breaking and entering," Feister told her.

"I don't care. I want to find my boy."

"We'll find him."

Debra's voice rose. "Don't say that! You don't know where to look. Nobody does. I want to find him before it's too late. Doesn't anybody understand that?"

Both officers spoke at once. Feister said, "Take it easy, ma'am," while Ottleson barked something about hysterics not helping.

"It's not your child," Debra reminded them. "It's mine. I know you're doing your job, but it's not enough."

"I've got kids of my own," said Feister.

What did he know? His children were safe at home. It was easy to sympathize, or say he did, but this was happening to her. To Drew.

"It's going to be too late," she whimpered.

CHAPTER 22

Home at last, Kurt thought. He should not have been driving in his condition, but it seemed stupid to call a taxi. Anyway, he made it. There wasn't too much traffic on a night like this.

Every light in the house was blazing. It hurt his eyes. It hurt him even worse to think of the electric bill. She was probably afraid to be left alone. She ought to be used to it by now, but maybe she wasn't used to this place. He'd have to remind her not to waste money. He'd tell her tomorrow, when he was sober.

As he got out of the car, a light came bobbing toward him. He was probably seeing things. Lights going off in his head.

"Gillis?" said a voice in the wind. It was Frank Maul, carrying a flashlight.

Frank gestured toward his own house. "You'd better come in here for a minute."

"Gotta go turn off those lights," said Kurt. He hoped he was making sense. He hoped the wind was blowing away his whiskey breath. There was something about alcohol fumes that damaged both a person's credibility and his dignity.

"Before you go in," Frank said firmly, "we have to tell you what's happening."

"Something's happening?"

"A lot. Come on in. Then you can decide what you want to do about it. If you can do anything."

Referring to his whiskey breath.

Kurt followed him up a brick walk, past some scratchy roses, and into the cottage, which he had never seen before. His first impression was one of coziness, but the lights were too bright. He saw an ash-blond woman of middle years and a young man in a wheelchair.

"You haven't met my wife, have you?" asked Frank. "This is Kurt Gillis. My wife Enid, my son Bill."

Kurt nodded to them and waited for the news to break. Had there been a fire? It didn't look that way. An accident? A burglary?

"Have a seat," said Frank, and almost pushed him into an armchair. "I said a lot's been going on, and it has. First I have to tell you that your daughter's in the hospital."

"Why?" asked Kurt. "Gigi? What for?" He thought he was managing very well, and maybe not sounding too stupid.

"Seems she wanted to go swimming," Frank explained, "and the surf was very strong. She might have been given a drug."

"Oh, hell." It flashed through Kurt's mind that he should have left Gigi on Long Island with her mother.

But Maul wasn't finished.

"Seems she told your wife what she was planning," he said. "Your wife went out to try and get her back. She left the boy alone with the house all locked up, but the kid disappeared. They're out looking for him now. The police."

"How could he get out if the house was locked?" asked Kurt.

"He's probably still there, then, isn't he?"

He wished Frank would slow down and let him grasp it all.

"He got out because somebody took him out," said Frank. "According to my son, it was Todd Jorgenson."

"Billy went to bed early," the wife put in. "His windows face that way. He saw Todd with your little boy."

"He was trying to tell us something," said Frank.

"Something about Todd," added the wife. "But he doesn't have the words. Todd was the one who shot Billy."

Kurt ran a hand through his usually impeccable hair. It was messed up by the wind anyway. He didn't understand what was going on.

"So why are the lights on?" he asked.

"Probably your wife looked through the house first," Enid Maul replied. "Then, when she couldn't find him, she came over here. We called the police. She's out now with the police."

"So nobody's home?"

"Nobody's home. I think she tried to call you."

"Probably." It would be like Debra. She had no faith in her own ability to handle things. He wished he could pull himself together and play the strong man now.

"Maybe I should go out," he suggested.

"I don't think so," said Frank. "You shouldn't be driving."

Kurt's dander was up. "I got myself home."

"Pure luck." Frank added a bit reluctantly, "I could go out with you. I could drive and you can look."

Enid cried, "You promised you'd stay in case he came here!"

"That's right," Frank agreed. "I did."

"Let me make you some coffee," she told Kurt. "If you wait a little, maybe you'll feel better."

"I feel fine," he said.

"It's deceptive." Frank talked as if he knew.

They were making him feel like a jerk, but he couldn't

argue. He knew there were tough laws against drunk driving. He should have stayed where he was, blissfully unaware.

"Why'd she have to go out and leave the kid?" he demanded. "That's not like her. She'd give her life for that kid. Sometimes I think she's crazy."

"She nearly gave her life for *your* kid," Frank informed him. "I happened to see them and I fished them both out. They were all but gone. The girl wasn't breathing."

"Oh, God, she's going to be brain-damaged."

"You don't know. Maybe not." Frank glanced at his son, who *was* brain-damaged. Then he reached over and patted the boy's arm. Enid turned away quickly, as though in tears.

Kurt went over what the Mauls had told him. He still didn't understand it all.

"What did Todd want with my kid?" he asked.

Billy Maul seemed to come to life. His hands worked furiously, trying to speak.

"He has aphasia," Frank explained. "He can't use words."

"He will," said Enid. "Give him time. What is it, honey?"

The boy had given up and sat slumped in his chair.

"You mean you know what Todd was doing?" Frank asked him.

Billy nodded. It was not a definite nod, and his face looked uncertain.

"If he has aphasia," said Kurt, "how come he can understand words?"

"Well, he can," replied Enid. "He just can't talk. What were you trying to say, dear?"

Billy shook his head. He seemed depressed. It was too much to try to explain. Maybe too complex an idea.

There was only one thing Kurt could think of. He hoped it wasn't that.

Billy looked around at them all, seeming to feel he must

make an effort. He pointed to his head. He opened his mouth and came out with a syllable that sounded like a croak.

"Todd shot you," said his mother.

Billy nodded. He reached down and held his hand with the palm just above the floor.

"Little kid?" asked Enid. Billy started to nod, when she added, "The Gillis boy?"

The nod turned to a shake of the head.

"Not the Gillis boy? Another little kid?"

Billy nodded approvingly. She had gotten it right.

"Hey, wait," she cried. "Just before you were shot—there was another little kid . . ."

Billy held his hand poised in the air. He made a beckoning gesture. Encouraging her.

"The Rinzler boy? The one they found on the beach?"

Billy nodded. Then he looked worried and his eyes darted back and forth.

"Todd had something to do with that?"

Another nod. The eyes widened. Billy pointed to his head.

"You knew about it?" asked Frank. "You mean that's why he shot you?"

An affirmative nod. But the worried expression remained.

"No wonder he said he was going to come and—" Enid clapped her hand to her mouth.

"I guess Billy's the key to this," she said, and looked at them all.

"So where's my kid?" demanded Kurt.

Billy blinked as though he had just been wakened. He tried to shrug.

"He doesn't know," said Enid.

Kurt would keep them all on track. "Well, what about the first kid, if Todd was responsible for that? What happened there? You seem to think it might have something to do with this." He was addressing Billy.

The boy drooped. He looked discouraged.

"Do you mean it's too hard to get across?" asked Kurt.

"Try it," said Enid. "We'll play Twenty Questions again."

Billy took a deep breath. He pointed to his father's chest.

"Dad?" asked Enid.

Billy nodded, but that was not all.

"Something to do with Dad?"

"It's got nothing to do with me," Frank said quickly.

Billy shook his head, but pointed again to his father. He made a gesture involving his arms and shoulders. It was not at all clear. Kurt noticed that his left side was stiffer than his right. He could scarcely move his left arm and shoulder.

"Try it again, honey," said Enid.

Billy tried it again. And again. His arms, bent at the elbows, made a circle that seemed to go over his shoulders.

"Put on?"

He shook his head and once again pointed to his father.

"Put on . . . Dad?"

A very frustrated shake of the head. The gestures grew more rapid. Billy patted his torso down to his hips. He pointed to his father and repeated the patting.

"Wait a minute . . ." Enid tried to think.

"I don't understand," said Frank.

"Something of Dad's?"

Billy nodded yes. Once more he showed them the patting. The gesture of putting on.

"Dad's . . . wait a minute. Dad's jacket?"

Yes! Yes!

"What about it, honey?"

Billy simply stared at his mother. She had forgotten to play Twenty Questions.

"Dad's jacket. Okay. Um—"

Kurt said, "I don't think this is helping to find my son."

Enid motioned him to be quiet as Billy pointed to the bedroom. Kurt was maddened. They had somehow connected Drew with the child who was found dead, but no one seemed able to take it from there.

"Go get Dad's jacket?" asked Enid. Billy nodded.

"The one he wears to work?"

Another nod.

Enid went to the bedroom. "Where is it, hon?" she called.

"Hanging on the door," Frank answered gloomily.

"I've got it."

She came back with a dark blue jacket and held it out to Billy.

He fumbled through it with his right hand. The better one. She helped him turn the jacket over. He reached into the breast pocket and took out something black.

"Dad's business cards?" asked Enid in bewilderment.

Billy pointed to the cards. Pointed to his father. Enid was stumped. Billy pantomimed driving a car.

"Oh, wait," said Enid.

"My office?" asked Frank.

Billy nodded.

"What about my office?"

Billy fumbled again. He could not seem to find what he wanted. He held out his hand and rubbed his thumb against his fingers.

"Money?" asked Frank. It was a standard gesture.

"Jesus," said Kurt. If Billy could do all that, why couldn't he say the words?

"The money in my office?" Frank seemed puzzled. Billy shook his head.

"Then what?"

Billy described with his hands two separate entities. That

was all Kurt could think of. Two entities. Billy pointed to the air where one had been, and then to the packet of business cards.

"My office," said Frank.

He had guessed correctly. Billy's hands moved back to the other entity.

"Near my—" Frank began. Again Billy made the beckoning gesture. Frank almost had it.

"Near my—next to my—next to my office? The *bank*?"

Billy nodded excitedly. Frank look flustered. His eyes darted to Enid and quickly away. She remained impassive.

"The bank," he repeated.

Billy's face began to work. He struggled to utter his only syllable.

"Dud."

"Todd?" said Enid. "The bank?"

Billy pantomimed taking things and putting them into a container which he held in his clumsy left hand.

"Take?" said Enid. "Take? Steal? Rob the bank?"

Yes! Yes! Yes!

"Todd? Rob the bank? But—"

Billy held his hand above the floor. The gesture for a small child. Then he pointed high above his head.

"Rob the bank?" Enid repeated. "A child? Rob the bank?"

Billy held his fingers to indicate something small and again pointed above his head.

"Hey. Yeah," exclaimed Frank. "Those little windows up at the top in back. Is that what you mean?"

Yes!

"He used a little kid? To get through the window? And open the door for him?"

Yes!

"How could he get up there?" Frank wanted to know.

"The tree!" said Enid. "There's a tree outside."

"It doesn't go up that high."

"He could have used something," she said. "A ladder, maybe."

Billy nodded.

"A ladder? From the tree?" Enid sounded incredulous. "He made a little kid go up . . . Oh, God."

"Oh, God," echoed Kurt.

"How do you know this?" asked Enid.

Kurt started up. Frank grabbed his arm.

"Let me go!" Kurt cried hoarsely. "The other kid broke his neck."

"Get the police," Frank told his wife. He kept his grip on Kurt. "They know how to handle this. They're closer anyway."

Kurt shouted, "It's my kid!"

"I know. I know."

Enid was calling the police. Kurt looked over at Billy.

"How do you know that? Were you in on it?"

Billy shook his head and pointed to his eyes.

"You saw it?"

Billy nodded, pantomimed driving a car, and pointed to his father. He pointed to the business cards.

"My parking lot," said Frank. "He must have gone into my parking lot. I said he could use it at night when nobody's there. Did Todd know you saw him?"

Billy shook his head.

"But he knew later."

Billy looked down at the floor.

"Okay," Frank said softly. But he could not resist adding, "You should have gone to the police."

"I got them," said Enid. "I told them."

Kurt sat down. He felt thoroughly drained. His head was still fuzzy from the drink. At the same time he had a sharp and painful awareness that he wished he could drown in more drink.

"Maybe they're still inside the bank," Enid told him kindly.

"Maybe it's too late," he said.

CHAPTER 23

They were cruising back along Barton Avenue. Debra saw the park brilliantly illuminated. They were searching it and the beach. But she still thought they were wrong.

"Will you let me out at my house?" she asked.

"Sure, if you want." Ottleson sounded almost taunting. Did she think this was funny?

"It would help if you were with us," said Feister.

"I know." Debra couldn't tell them what she meant to do.

"But there aren't many small children out tonight, are there? If you see one . . . He was wearing yellow pajamas." Her throat became choked. "With ducks. White ducks."

"Could be wearing something over it," Ottleson said matter-of-factly.

"Yes. He could be."

And barefooted. Would Todd have bothered to put shoes on him? She hadn't checked to see if his shoes were there. His little red sneakers.

They turned in at her driveway. They took her right to the door.

All the lights were still on. She hadn't turned them off after her mad, desperate search.

Then she noticed Kurt's car. So he had finally come home. Was he in the house, wondering?

She didn't stop to look. She didn't even wait until the police car had turned around and driven away.

Instead she walked quickly up the driveway. After a moment she noticed that the wind was not as strong as before.

She hurried past the picket fence and into Mrs. Maul's garden. Their lights were on, too, as before. She didn't pause, but went out through the gate onto Angel Road. She could have asked the police to leave her at the corner, but she hadn't wanted them to know what she planned to do.

The Jorgenson house was still dark, except for the porch light. For a moment she allowed herself to be bathed in it, spotlighted, while she rang the doorbell.

She rang repeatedly, listening to the chimes play their frantic *ping pong* inside the house. When she was sure no one would answer, she went around to the back door, where she could not be seen so easily from the street.

Todd's car was still there. It was the only one. They might have gone somewhere together, in Hazel's car.

She wavered. Maybe they were out for a perfectly innocent evening, and the Mauls were lying. Covering up for Billy.

Or maybe Todd was there in the house. That was what she had to find out.

She had never been at the house before. Never been in back of it. She was relieved to see that the door did indeed have a window.

She rang the back doorbell and rapped on the glass. She

peered through it, but could see nothing in the darkened room.

Then she scuffed about, wondering how she could have been so stupid. It was a small lot, and neatly kept. Why would there be a rock on it?

There wasn't. The parking area was paved and there was a tiny, grassy backyard. She could see all that and not much else in the dim earthlight.

And she was barefooted. Not even a shoe.

She looked up at the sky, at the blowing clouds. She saw darkness and light. She watched for increasing brightness in one spot.

For an instant the moon was clear, casting its light around her. Beside the back step she saw two plastic flowerpots, one with dirt in it. She picked it up.

Her first try was tentative. It went against her grain to break someone else's window.

But she had to find Drew. A search warrant could take well into tomorrow. She swung again.

The glass shattered. She heard it hit the floor. She listened for sounds inside the house, then carefully reached her arm through the hole she had made.

She groped for the door lock. It was a button that turned inside the knob. She twisted it to a horizontal position and opened the door.

The kitchen was pitch-dark and unfamiliar. There should have been a switch near the door. There was always a switch near a door. She ran her hand over the wall until she found it and turned it on.

It was the outside light, and it sent an amber glow through the window. It showed, over in a corner near the refrigerator, something lying on the floor.

Now she could see the other switch. The one that lit the

room. She knew she had to turn it on.

It came dimly at first. A fluorescent flicker. The next instant, the room was ablaze.

Debra backed toward the door. She looked quickly to see if anyone was coming. Whether anyone had heard her.

And then, not knowing quite what she was doing, she ran.

CHAPTER 24

It was no wonder Billy hadn't wanted to come home, Enid thought. He was afraid of Todd. And his anger with her was because she had insisted.

Kurt was fidgeting. "What about that bank?"

Enid said, "You might as well stay here. The police are already checking. Do you want me to call them?"

He set down his coffee cup. "I feel better already. I can drive."

"No, you can't," Frank told him. "Coffee doesn't really help. It doesn't clear your blood."

"What do you expect me to *do*?" Kurt sounded furious.

"I expect you to wait," Frank replied. "The police'll tell us if they find him. Enid, go call the police."

"I don't like to tie up their lines," she muttered, in an attempt to assert herself. She went to the kitchen and called, not their emergency number, but the regular one.

Returning to the living room, she announced, "They don't have any reports of finding anything at the bank."

Billy looked crestfallen. Her heart went out to him.

"You could have been right, honey," she told him. "Maybe he left already."

Frank asked, "Did he get inside the bank?"

"They didn't say. You know they don't tell you anything when they're investigating."

"If he didn't," Kurt began. "If he didn't . . ." He ground his fist against his forehead. "How can they find him? He could have gone anywhere. And he's getting farther away."

There was a thundering at the door. Before Enid could reach it, it flew open.

The Gillis woman stood there, as frowsled and barefooted as she had been earlier. Her eyes were wild.

"Debra!" Kurt exclaimed, rising from his chair.

Debra cried hoarsely, "She's dead!"

"Who?"

"Hazel Jorgenson. She's dead on the kitchen floor. I saw her."

"How did you—"

"I broke in. The police wouldn't do it till they get a search warrant, but I thought Drew might be there." She began to cry.

Enid felt something twist inside her. It was tough being a mother.

She glanced at Billy. At least she still had him, or what was left of him. From now on it couldn't get worse. Only better.

"You broke into the house?" Kurt was asking. "How?"

Debra explained, sobbing, "I broke a window. It's very easy, breaking into a house. You're just not supposed to."

Frank had reached the kitchen in two strides. Enid saw him pick up the phone.

"How do you call the police?" he asked.

Enid told him. She could not believe what she had heard. She could not believe it even enough to think of calling the police herself.

"Hazel?" she asked.

"I saw her," Debra repeated.

"What happened?"

"I don't know. I saw blood. Then I ran."

"Are you sure she was dead?" asked Kurt.

Debra groaned. "Her eyes were open."

The whole thing began to reach Kurt, too. "What if Todd was there? Are you out of your mind?"

"Yes!" Debra cried. "I've been out of my mind all night! Ever since your daughter tried to drown herself."

"If she was drugged," said Kurt, "he might have given it to her. To get you both out of the way. Or distract you."

She covered her face with her hands. "They can't find him."

Enid helped her into a chair. "Have some coffee." What the woman really needed was a sedative.

"I don't know why they took him," Debra wept.

"Billy might—" Enid began, then stopped herself. She glanced at Kurt, who shook his head. Debra was not to know.

Enid handed her a cup of coffee, but Debra ignored it.

"I have to go look for him," she insisted. "Kurt, what are you doing here?"

"I can't drive," he admitted sheepishly.

"If you'd been home—" she accused.

"I know." He spoke with a gentle smile. "Then I would have been the one to go. Gigi and I would both be drowned by now, but you and Drew would be safe."

"I don't care about *me*." She jumped up. "I have to go. Where are the car keys?"

"You can't," he said. "You're in no better shape than I am."

"I could drive you," said Enid, "if Frank stays here. Frank's got to stay here."

She was surprised at herself. She hated the woman. Perhaps not now, but she still did not like her.

Debra was saying, "Would you? I can't just sit here."

"I thought you were out with the police," said Enid.

"I made them drop me off. I had to see in that house."

"You don't even know where to look," Kurt reminded them both.

"Neither do the police," Debra said.

Enid opened the coat closet and found a jacket.

"Here," she told Debra. "You must be frozen by now. Do you want some shoes?" Enid's feet were long and narrow. Debra's were smaller. Debra glanced in the direction of her own house and seemed to decide it would take too much time. Enid brought her a pair of sneakers. Her gardening shoes.

"Frank," she said, "you stay here with Billy. Don't you dare leave him, not for one second."

"Got it," said Frank.

The two women went out to Enid's car.

"Where do you want to start?" Enid asked.

Debra shook her head. She huddled, shivering, on the seat. "It's just that I can't sit there doing nothing."

"Let's see." Enid was the one who knew Todd better. But she didn't really know him at all, it seemed.

He had shot Billy. Ruined his life. For that, if nothing else, she wanted to find him. And Todd had better hope she didn't.

"Let's go check the house," she decided, and turned up Angel Road. "He might be there. Maybe he was lying low."

"He took her car," said Debra.

"How do you know?"

"It wasn't there."

The Jorgenson driveway and the curb outside it were ablaze with flashing lights. There was an ambulance with its back doors open. Police cars. She wondered if Hazel could still be alive.

She parked at the end of the block, which was as close as she could get, and hurried out of the car. She was vaguely aware of Debra following her.

A policeman tried to hold them back. Enid asked, "Is there anybody else in the house? Is the son there?"

"I don't know what's there," replied the officer, then narrowed his eyes. "What do you know about this?"

Enid wondered how much it would implicate Debra, but decided to level with him.

"This is the woman who found her. Todd Jorgenson kidnapped her little boy. She thought they might be in there."

Debra shivered in spite of Enid's jacket. They saw two men come out of the house carrying a stretcher. Enid pushed as far forward as she could.

"She's dead. Her face is covered," she reported to Debra. Poor Hazel, she thought, and felt sick.

"What do they think happened?" she asked the officer. Maybe it hadn't been Todd who killed her.

"Don't know yet." He wouldn't tell her even if he did.

Debra clutched at her arm. "He might be in there."

"We can't go in," said Enid, "but they're looking. See? They even have a light on in the basement."

"What am I going to do?"

"Sometimes you can't do anything," Enid told her. "Sometimes things just happen." She knew it was hardly comforting, but it was true.

Debra's voice rose. "I have to find my boy! Why aren't all these people out looking for him? Hazel's already dead."

She broke away and collared a tall officer who was sweeping a flashlight beam over the bushes and shrubbery. It was one of the two who had come to the house, Enid remembered.

She saw the man shake his head. Then they both came toward her. Before the man could speak, Debra was begging, "Can you give a description of Hazel's car? Please?"

"It's green," said Enid. "Kind of metallic green. I'm really no good at this."

"Light? Dark?" asked the officer.

"Dark, I guess. It's old. Not in very good condition. I mean, you can hardly see that it's metallic anymore."

"Do you know the make?"

"Oh, God. I know it's American. It's kind of big."

"Body type?"

"Sedan. Let's see. Two doors. I'm really not good at this. My husband—"

"You wouldn't happen to know the plate number."

"No, I'm sorry. But it's yellow. I remember that. It's one of those old yellow Jersey plates."

"That's a help. Thank you." The man went to one of the cars and sent a radio message.

"They'll put out a bulletin," said Enid.

"But maybe he's not in the car," Debra wept.

"It's a start, anyway. If they can find the car, then they'll know which way he went, maybe."

She still felt her old revulsion. But there was a softening, too. She gave in to it and put her arm around Debra's shoulders.

Debra collapsed against her, sobbing.

"I know, I know," said Enid. She did know, although her child had been lost in a different way.

And both because of Todd.

"Do you want to go on in the car?" she asked.

"I don't know what else to do," said Debra.

Enid tried to think. "I'm sure they checked the beach. And the park." Because of the other child, who had been found there.

"But what would he want with Drew?" Debra cried. "People like that . . . Don't they often kill them afterward?"

"You've got it wrong," Enid said gently. "From what Billy told us, it wasn't anything like that."

"Billy knows?" Debra's face closed again. It was the way she had looked when she first came over to the house, suspecting Billy.

"That's why he got shot," said Enid. "Because he saw." She would not tell the full story. "Todd did a lot of burglaries. He broke in places to steal, so he could buy drugs. Sometimes he couldn't get in. He had to send a little kid in through a small window to open the door for him."

"Drew wouldn't understand that!" Debra cried. "He's too little." Then she became eager. "Where would he try to break in?"

"They already looked," said Enid. "Where Billy saw the other one."

Maybe it was different this time, but she didn't think so. The bank would have been the most alluring place. And they probably didn't think to put burglar alarms on those high, small windows. Secretly she thought Drew was already dead of a broken neck, like the other child.

The bank where McCoy worked. Damn it, she did not want to remember McCoy.

"Let's go," she said, and took Debra by the arm.

"Go where?" Debra asked hopelessly.

"I don't know. Maybe some of the other banks. I just don't know."

CHAPTER 25

Todd drove back and forth, looking for a place to dump the body. It was in the trunk of his car, along with the folding ladder. The ladder by itself was innocent enough. If they stopped him, he could say he had a job cleaning gutters.

But they had no reason to stop him. Unless they happened to notice how badly the car was spray-painted. There hadn't been time to do a decent job. It was streaked and splotchy.

And then she had caught him at it. That was the worst part. He thought he was a goner then. The bossy, meddling old idiot.

He drove back and forth past rows of small old houses. He had been there with Gigi. Ages ago. If he could get down to the beach where they'd gone that night . . .

Last night? Was it only *last night*?

But there were too many cars around. Police cars, too. If he could just slip out of town . . . Still, it was pretty far to reach any real countryside. That whole stretch along the shore was one town after another.

He began to wish he hadn't put the body in the trunk. If he had it beside him, he could just open a door and throw it out. But when he'd had to flee the bank, he thought it was better to have everything hidden.

Probably by now they'd found the kid missing. But they wouldn't know how. Or where. Unless somebody'd seen him. He didn't see how anybody could, except from the Maul house. But their living-room lights had been on. When you look out from a lighted room into the dark, you can't see anything.

Bill might remember that other time. But he couldn't talk. Gigi had said so. Besides, if he was brain-damaged, he probably couldn't remember. Or, if he did, how could he put it all together?

Every one of those houses had a driveway. Now all he needed was an empty house . . . But if somebody saw a car going in, they'd get suspicious. He switched off his lights.

Then he cruised half a block, looking for the right place.

There was a good one. Tree-shaded. The house next to it was empty, too. He was about to turn in when another car came up the street.

It flashed its lights at him. As it passed, a man leaned from the window.

"Turn 'em on, buddy."

"Oh. Thanks," said Todd.

He cursed to himself. That did it. If the kid were found there, that man might just happen to remember.

He put the lights back on and continued driving. He'd have to find another place. Hell. Maybe he should dump the whole car.

That idea lasted only an instant. Unless he could dump it where nobody'd find it, ever, they could trace it back to his mother with the dead kid in it. Besides, he'd paid more than a hundred dollars for the ladder. It worked great on two-story houses, but not the damned bank.

There were more houses with lights on in the next street. Terrific. He was running out of places. Better just to ditch the kid somewhere. He picked up speed, turning corners—but not fast enough to draw attention—until he reached the K-mart plaza.

K-mart was closed now, but a few other stores were open and there were still some cars around. He found an out-of-the-way corner near the garden shop. Tall white lights illuminated the entire plaza. He parked next to a chain-link fence, angling the car so no one could see him.

He felt himself getting low. That was no good when he needed all his faculties. Luckily he had a little coke. Hadn't dared bring too much. He thought of that big stash at home. He could sneak back there after he dumped the kid. And it would have to be soon. Once they found his mother's body, they'd be all over the place.

His supply was in a plastic folder with the maps and stuff. They wouldn't have found it unless they really looked. He snorted a little and put back the rest. Enough for one more time, maybe.

Then he got to work. He opened the trunk. Under the ladder was an old bedspread his mother kept for padding in case she carried something scratchable. He could put the kid in that. He got it all arranged, then reached for the body.

The kid felt cold, but he wasn't stiff. Todd didn't know how long it took before stiffness set in. He was glad it hadn't yet. He wouldn't have liked that. He wrapped the body and placed it on the front seat. It was risky, but easier to toss it out if he came to a good place.

He'd have to go home. Had to get that stuff. It wouldn't take long. It was all in the basement. After he got it, he'd figure out what to do with it. Hide it somewhere in the car. Maybe a door panel. He could drive all night, but then he'd have to ditch the car. It was too badly painted. They'd see that in the daylight.

The airport was out. It would have been the best bet, but they'd find his stuff and haul him in, and that would open an even bigger can of worms. No good. He'd pictured himself with a lot of money, no dead kid, and no dead old lady back home. How could it have gone so wrong?

He headed for home. They wouldn't have found her yet. No reason to. He'd left only the front light on, as if she was out, and her car, of course, was gone. Nobody'd wonder about him. If they saw his car there, they'd just think he got picked up by some friends to go somewhere. He did have friends. A few.

It was a five-minute drive across town, including traffic lights. There weren't too many cars around. The wind was still blowing but not as much. It could be a good day tomorrow. Good for Luna Beach. But he wouldn't be there.

As he turned onto Angel Road, he saw flashing lights in the distance. Oh, hell. Shit.

He thought of turning off. But maybe it wasn't that. Maybe it was somebody having a heart attack.

He drove on. Slowly. The light was on his side of the street. On his block, he thought.

It was. He reached the block that had the old grave. The light was on the next one. Right in the middle, where his house was. A lot of flashing lights, not just one. They always left those things spinning.

The grave. He slowed down. It was dark in there. How far could he throw this thing?

God, a two-year-old kid. It weighed a ton. He'd really thought of just dumping it out along the roadside, into a ditch, but there weren't any ditches in the middle of town.

He stopped the car. There were houses here, but he didn't see any people. They were probably all down there gaping at his old lady.

He got out of the car, ran around to the other side, and picked up the bundle.

Even at the railing, he realized he couldn't throw it. He wanted it back under those trees. Out of sight. He jumped over the rail.

Maybe not all the way back. The grave was good enough, under that willow tree. He dumped it between the headstone and the tree trunk, and then ran back to his car.

He didn't think anybody'd seen him. He was safe. There wasn't any blood in the car.

He thought of turning off at the next block. But he had to see. He really had to see what they were doing. They wouldn't recognize him. Not with white paint on the car. Even a bad job of it.

It was the drug that gave him so much gall. He knew that. It seemed to lift him by the head and pull him forward. He laughed aloud, thinking of all that consternation in there.

He slowed down as an ambulance pulled out of the driveway. An *ambulance*? It gave him a scare, until he realized it was probably routine. They'd use an ambulance even if she was dead, just to make sure.

There were police all over the place. He'd have to drive on past and leave his wonderful stash. And he didn't have the money to get much more, thanks to that dumb kid.

He passed a car at the curb. It looked like Enid Maul's car, but he didn't think much about it. She'd probably come to see what was happening.

There was the Gillis place with all its lights on. They must have discovered the kid was missing. He almost forgot about the Mauls' little house until he was level with it and saw them out in front. He saw the old man and Gigi's father and some guy in a wheelchair.

God. Billy. They were helping him into a car. He didn't think Billy could have talked. Gigi said he couldn't talk.

What did he know? He hadn't seen. But he knew about the other kid.

It all raced through Todd's mind as he saw them there. In another second or two, Billy would be inside the car. He couldn't have talked. But he might. Oh, God, he might.

Todd fumbled under the seat. It was there. His gun. Shit, the window was closed. He opened it quickly. He pointed the gun at Billy's head and fired.

CHAPTER 26

"It's Todd!" Debra cried. "That was Todd!"
"Where?" asked Enid.
"In that car. The white one."

Enid knew which one. It had slowed briefly in front of her house. All she really saw was her family. Getting into the car. After the white car slowed, they suddenly speeded up. Billy was rushed into the back seat, the other two men scrambled inside, the doors all closed. She saw the car spring to life as its lights went on, and it wheeled around and started down the driveway.

Todd doesn't have a white car, she was thinking, but her foot pressed the accelerator. The white car turned right on Barton Avenue. Enid spun after it. She was aware of Frank hurtling down the driveway on her right.

"What happened?" she asked.
"Please," moaned Debra. "He has my child."

Enid knew she could never keep up with him. Young men were accustomed to driving fast. It was why they had such a high accident rate. All she thought about was not letting him out of her sight. Not letting any other cars come between.

Someone was on her tail. She glanced in the mirror. It was Frank.

"They're behind us," she said. "Your husband and Frank."

Debra said nothing. She leaned forward, staring ahead. Keeping Todd's car fixed with her eyes. Enid saw the yellow license plate. There were still some around, although for a number of years all the new issues had been blue. There were far more blue ones than yellow.

"He must have painted the car," she said.

Debra moaned again. "Please. Oh, God."

"Look," said Enid, "if we make him too nervous, he might crash."

Todd sped through an amber traffic light. Enid did not hesitate. Frank came after her. A car in the intersection blew its horn.

"I don't care," Enid muttered. She remembered that Frank always scolded her for going through amber lights at wide intersections, although he did it himself. Now they were together.

He's with me, she thought. Suddenly Marianne McCoy flashed through her mind. Frank said he had been thinking there on the beach. What had he thought?

The next light glared red. Todd drove straight through it. Enid barely slowed. "Watch the right," she snapped, and looked both ways.

Frank was still behind her.

At the next corner, Todd made a sudden right. Enid's tires squealed as she turned after him. She had no time to signal, but Frank followed.

They were on a narrow street. She was vaguely aware of a truck coming toward them when Todd made a quick left.

She had to wait for the truck. Then she followed. Todd was nearly out of sight, turning left again. Zigzagging, to lose her. Enid picked up speed.

There was a bar on the corner. She saw people leave it and start across the street. She blew her horn. They stared at her furiously. One man made an obscene gesture. She couldn't see whether Frank was still there.

She had lost Todd.

"Right," said Debra. "He went right."

Enid turned right. She didn't see him.

"Oh, God," Debra cried again.

Enid had nearly passed the next street when, a block away on her left, she saw a taillight whipping around a corner. She made an abrupt and clumsy turn. Doing so, she caught a glimpse of Frank behind her.

Todd had been turning right. She saw him now, making another left. And another. Always a block ahead.

Back to Barton Avenue. She understood now. He was trying to get out to the highway.

"Damn, if we just had a radio," she said.

"There were all those police," Debra sobbed. "Why didn't they follow?"

A red traffic light ahead. Barton Avenue. She knew which way he was going. She turned right. There was no time to look in the mirror. To see Frank.

She saw Todd ahead in the left lane. Several cars were between them. She wove in and out, passing them.

Todd sailed into the right lane and made a quick right turn.

A car was on her right.

It was Frank. He sped after Todd and so did she.

Todd was trying to get out of the shoreline metropolis. And then what? He couldn't be aiming for the parkway. It had tolls. He would have to slow for them.

She lowered her foot almost to the floor. Couldn't look at the speedometer. Her mind became a single idea. Todd. It tied her to his car like a tow rope.

He meant to lose her in the darkness. No way. She could not remember why she wanted him. All she knew was keeping him in sight.

It was a four-lane road. Todd was in the right. She saw taillights ahead and moved to the left. She would block him from passing.

She drove faster. Still faster.

Now she could see his face. Next to her. It was dark, but she saw Todd.

He looked at her. He had caught up with the slow car but couldn't pass. She was in his way.

She could cut him off. She pulled slightly ahead. A horn blasted just behind her.

It was Frank. He was in back of Todd.

She would force Todd off the road.

"He says no," Debra told her.

"Who says?"

"Your husband." Debra's voice became a gurgle. "Look out, he has a gun!"

Enid ducked her head. Her car smashed against Todd's and bounced off it. The impact sent her careening.

She did not know what she was doing. Spinning through the night. The window on Debra's side was broken.

"Are you all right?" Enid asked.

"He's shooting!" screamed Debra. "And he's got my baby!"

Enid straightened the car. She was still moving ahead. But Todd had gotten away. And Frank.

A light caught her eye. In the mirror. A flashing light.

"They're coming," she said.

Maybe chasing her. She slowed. Todd had broken her

concentration. She pulled to the side of the road.

Just ahead of her there were taillights crazily on the shoulder. And the sound of gunfire.

She had done it. Knocked Todd off the road. She leaned forward on her steering wheel, weak and shaking, as a dwindling siren passed her and stopped just ahead.

CHAPTER 27

Todd laughed at the silliness of it all. "What kid?" He chuckled, turning on his charm. "What would I be doing with a kid? Here, be my guests." Gallantly he waved them toward his car.

The police asked him to open the trunk. It contained odds and ends of tools and implements, and a folding ladder. They asked him what the ladder was for.

"Business," he said. "I'm a freelance gutter cleaner. It's the only job I could get."

"Okay, young man. You have the right to remain silent . . ."

"Hey, what is this? Just for having a ladder in my car?"

"Concealed weapon, reckless endangerment, suspicion of homicide . . . You name it. You have the right to remain silent. Anything you say—"

"Where's my baby?" Debra cried. She went over to Frank's car and pounded on the glass beside Billy. "Where's my baby?"

"Wait a minute," said Enid. "He hasn't got your baby."

"He said it was Todd, but Todd doesn't ha—"

Enid seized her arm. "You believe Todd after all this? Maybe because he's so good-looking, and Billy's crippled? Is that it?"

She still felt the bitterness, even knowing that Billy hadn't shot himself. It would stay with her for a long, long time. She started back to her car.

Frank called, "Where are you going?"

"To find that kid." She spoke with no urgency. The child was dead. She noticed that her passenger door was smashed in. She had done it herself, knocking Todd off the road. They might not have caught him if she hadn't done that and he hadn't taken the trouble to fire at her.

"Figure it," she told Debra, who had to climb in first from the driver's side because the other door would not open. "Todd had your son. I believe Billy even if you don't. He had him and he doesn't have him now, so he's somewhere back in town."

Frank was going back, too, and so were the police, although the car with Todd in it would have to head for the jail. She did feel satisfied about that.

"Poor Hazel," she said. Debra took no notice. But what had gone wrong? Hazel was so sure she had the answers. Maybe nobody had them.

Maybe Hazel hadn't loved him enough, in spite of the fuss over homework. Maybe too much love was better than not enough. Or whatever. It wasn't easy, raising a child.

She glanced at Debra. All that was over for her now.

They went first to the bank, although she knew the police had been there. She did not know where else to look.

They combed the area with a flashlight from her glove compartment, peering into cellar window wells and every nook and cranny of the parking lot.

They crossed the street to the luncheonette and looked in the dumpster out in the back. Debra was crying audibly. The police came with more powerful lanterns and searched the same area.

"Did you guys check the beach?" Enid asked them.

"All over," they said.

"All those empty houses? He was probably the one who did a lot of those burglaries."

"They're going through those now," the officers replied.

"Well, then . . ."

Debra clutched at her arm.

"He passed us when we were at his house. He went right past there on Angel Road."

"But where did he go before that?" Enid asked her. "That was quite a time lapse."

"I want to look there."

"At his house? He didn't get out of his car. And the police were all over it."

"No, before that. He took Gigi to see it. That grave. It seemed to have some weird fascination for him. Oh, my God. He asked how old Drew was, and . . . Oh, God."

Enid told the police where they were going. "Just in case," she added. "I think he would have ditched it before that."

"Hurry," said Debra as Enid started the car. "Oh, he's got to be somewhere."

"That's right." Enid knew it relieved people's minds even to know someone was dead. It was better than not knowing anything.

Billy's first night home, she thought. And then she realized that Todd must have fired at Billy when he passed them at the house. And evidently missed.

Poor Billy. If only he could have told her about Todd.

She waited for a traffic light. Debra closed her eyes and leaned back her head as though trying to endure the delay. Trying to stop time.

"How much farther is it?" she asked.

"Just a few blocks." Enid drove as fast as she dared.

208

Another traffic light. Debra moaned.

Enid looked back and saw Frank's car.

"They're coming," she said. Probably they thought she was going home.

Debra clenched her hands. "I shouldn't have gone out to get Gigi."

"What else could you do?" Enid asked.

"I traded Drew's life for hers."

"But how could you know?"

"I wish I'd died there in the water. I wish your husband hadn't come along . . ."

"I was thinking of dying, too," said Enid. If she had, she would have failed Billy.

The next light was yellow. She sped through it. Frank stopped and she left him behind.

She turned the corner onto Angel Road. There were no traffic lights there. She drove two blocks and stopped by the grave.

"There are houses all around," she said. "They would have seen if anybody was doing anything."

But it was dark and the willow tree cast a shadow. She got out of the car and let Debra out.

"I see something!" Debra cried. Something blowing. It could have been anything. Young people sometimes held trysts there, and could have shed a garment or two.

They hurried over the rail and across the grass. Then Enid stood back as Debra crouched over the whipping bundle of cloth.

"No!" cried Debra. "Oh, no. No."

Then Frank and Kurt were there. Kurt bent down and felt the bundle.

"He's alive. Barely. Call an ambulance."

"There's no time!" Debra gathered up her child.

"Careful," said Kurt. "In case something's broken."

"She knows to be careful," Enid snapped at him.

"Get in my car," said Frank. "We'll go to the hospital. Enid, you call them and tell them to get ready, okay?"

"He's so cold," Debra said over and over again. "So icy cold. His thin little pajamas . . ."

Enid ran toward her car. She saw lights down at the Jorgenson house. Some police were still there. It wouldn't take long.

Frank called after her, "We'll see you back at the house."

CHAPTER 28

"Daddy?" Gigi whimpered. "I'm sorry. Todd made me give him the key. I owed him so much money, and I didn't know where to get it, so I had to give him the key. I don't remember what happened after that."

"He didn't care if you died," Debra told her, noting that the apology was only to Kurt. "Or if I died. Or Drew."

"But you don't understand." Gigi's voice was weak and still hoarse from the water. "That's the way it is. The only thing that matters is coke. You have to get more. It's all that counts. He gave me so much and I owed him for it. And he owed somebody who was going to kill him if he didn't pay, so he had to get into the bank. Daddy, I want to get over it."

"You knew all that?" Debra asked.

"Yes, I knew. But I owed him. He wouldn't give me any more."

"You sold your brother for cocaine." Debra was filled with loathing.

"I couldn't help it," Gigi pleaded.

"God," said Kurt.

Gigi did not ask how Drew was. Debra went back to the small lounge on the third floor. She would wait there all night, seeing Drew for only five minutes every two hours. He was in intensive care.

He would make it, the doctors said. He had a concussion that had knocked him unconscious. He had a broken arm and three broken ribs. His very youth, they said, his light weight and the pliancy of his bones might have saved him from further injury. He had not broken his neck as the first child had who fell from Todd's ladder.

Kurt came into the lounge. "I'm going home and catch some sleep," he said. "They gave me a number to call a taxi. I'll stop by in the morning. You'll be okay?"

"Yes," said Debra. "I'll be okay."

As long as Drew was all right, she would be, too. Kurt could go and sleep anywhere he wanted. Even with Georgia Pietsch. It would probably always be like that.

But she had her child back, and that was what mattered. She curled into an armchair and prepared to spend a fitful night.

Together, Frank and Enid helped Billy into bed. He seemed relaxed, almost cheerful, now that Todd was locked up. He had actually smiled at them.

When they were alone in the living room, Enid asked, "Well, what did you decide?"

"About what?"

She peered into Frank's face. He really did not know what she meant.

"You were taking a lonely walk along the beach, thinking," she reminded him. "You said so."

"Oh. Yes, well, I was just thinking. It kind of blows my mind to think about that kid. But I guess it's going to be all hers, not mine. That's the way she wants it. She even has a guy who wants to marry her."

"Well, that's something. I hope the guy isn't you."

He looked sheepish. "No, it's not. There never was anything . . . It was just physical, that's all. And I'm sorry, Enid, for what I put you through."

What could she say? It had not helped much, considering what else she was going through. But it had not been the worst of her problems, either.

"Anyway, it's finished," he told her. "You know, I was really proud of you tonight. All those things you did. Figuring Billy out. Going after Todd—even if you did almost get yourself killed. You really brought it off."

"So what does that prove?" she asked.

"I'm proud of you, Enid. I love you."

Her eyes met his. This was Frank talking? He hadn't said those words in twenty years.

"I love you, too," she said, her lips forming a phrase that for her, as well, was rusty from disuse.

"We're going to be okay." He moved over onto the sofa beside her. "Don't you think so? We're going to be okay, and we're going to work together to help Billy get back as much as he can."

She didn't answer. She was starting to cry.

He understood. He slipped one arm around her and held her closely, while with the other hand he turned out the lamp.